SMOOTH OPERATOR

Clandestine Affairs 2

Zara Chase

MENAGE EVERLASTING

Siren Publishing, Inc.
www.SirenPublishing.com

A SIREN PUBLISHING BOOK
IMPRINT: Ménage Everlasting

SMOOTH OPERATORS
Copyright © 2013 by Zara Chase

ISBN: 978-1-62740-632-1

First Printing: November 2013

Cover design by Les Byerley
All art and logo copyright © 2013 by Siren Publishing, Inc.

Printed in U.S.A.

PUBLISHER
Siren Publishing, Inc.
www.SirenPublishing.com

SMOOTH OPERATORS

Clandestine Affairs 2

ZARA CHASE
Copyright © 2013

Chapter One

Raoul and Zeke galloped across the open prairie, heading back to their Wyoming ranch. The hands had done a decent job of repairing the fencing on the southern pasture, and they wouldn't be losing any more stock through that route. Raoul inhaled deeply. It felt good to be outside for a while. He spent way too much time closeted in his office, overseeing their clandestine operations organization that had grown out of control. He and Zeke had started out trying to fix a few problems for fellow ex-servicemen, and before they knew it, they had a full-blown business on their hands.

Zeke pulled his horse across Raoul's line, deliberately goading him, stirring his buddy's competitive spirit. He ought to have known better. Zeke might have been virtually born on the back of a horse, but Raoul was no slouch himself when it came to this stuff, and since Zeke was clearly fixing for a fight, Raoul was happy to oblige. Grinning, Raoul swung his horse to the left and then cut back in front of Zeke again, forcing him to swerve. With a clear line back to the barn, Raoul beat Zeke home by a full head.

"Shit, man, you don't play fair," Zeke complained, laughing as he slapped his horse's sweaty neck and dismounted.

"Listen to who's talking."

They unsaddled their horses and hosed them down. They might be the bosses, but it didn't occur to either of them to let someone else clean up after them.

"Good to see you haven't forgotten how to ride," Zeke said as they led their horses back out to the paddock.

"It's okay, partner. I won't tell that you got beat."

"Hah, only 'cause you cheated."

"Yeah, right."

"You fancy going into town tonight, hitting a few bars, see what's around?" Zeke asked.

Raoul knew what Zeke was suggesting. The two of them were into sharing their women, just like they shared most everything else about their lives. It had been a while since they'd found a female who met with their exacting standards, mainly because Raoul couldn't be bothered to look. Whenever he did go into town, the women tended to come on to him, which was an immediate turnoff. Raoul liked to be the one who did the pursuing.

"You go, buddy. I got some stuff I need to catch up with."

"Use it or lose it," Zeke said, grinning. "That cock of yours will drop off if it don't see some action soon. It's not as though you don't get any offers. What about the chick who runs the feed store in town? She's shit hot, and I don't think she'd turn either of us down, not if I'm reading the signals right."

"Yeah, I agree she's cute, but I can't work up any enthusiasm."

"You're regressing, buddy," Zeke said as they walked back to the house together. "I know you still miss her, but you have to move on."

Zeke was the only person who could talk to Raoul about his dead wife without running the risk of having his head removed from his shoulders. He'd been there, knew what had happened to Cantara, and had suffered right alongside Raoul when they were captured trying to save her. Zeke was right in one respect. Raoul *had* managed to live again for a while, if you could call it that. But it all seemed kinda pointless now—sex for the sake of it when his emotions weren't engaged.

The problem was that his emotions never would be engaged again. They'd died right alongside Cantara and their unborn child, and Raoul was good with that. He'd constructed some sort of barricade around the part of him that used to be able to feel because he never wanted to experience the searing pain of loss—the hopelessness that took him over when he failed to save the love of his life—ever again.

Zeke, on the other hand, firmly believed that life went on. Well, that was easy for him to say.

"Yeah, okay, we'll go into town tonight." Raoul slapped Zeke's shoulder. "Happy now?"

Zeke chuckled. "Delirious."

They both headed for Raoul's office, where Raoul immediately checked his secure email account—the one only a privileged few had access to—the one where requests for their particular services came in. There was only one new mail since Raoul had checked earlier. Surprised to recognize the sender's name and wondering what he could possibly need from Raoul, he immediately opened it.

"Take a look at this," he said.

Zeke peered over Raoul's shoulder. "From Major Redmond. Thought he was still in Iraq."

"He is and he wants to talk to us over the secure line."

"Must be something important. He's not the type to panic about stuff."

Raoul shrugged. "What's the time over there now?"

"They're nine hours ahead. He said he'd called when he got off this evening, so I guess that could be anytime now."

The call came almost an hour later.

"Major, nice to hear from you," Raoul said, not wasting time with small talk. "What can I do for you?"

"I'm not sure that you can, son, but I sure as hell need some help from somebody. There's fuck all I can do about the situation back at home while I'm stuck in this hellhole."

"Best tell us about it. Zeke's here and you're on speaker phone."

"Hey, Major," Zeke said. "Good talking with you."

"You, too." The major paused. "My problem is with my little gal."

"Your daughter?"

"Right, only I guess Briana's not so little anymore. She's twenty-four now, and just about as independent as they come, but she'll always be a baby to me."

"What's she done to get you worried enough to call us?" Zeke asked.

"Well, that's just it, I'm not exactly sure, and it's driving me crazy."

"Start at the beginning, sir," Raoul said.

"Okay, she majored in marine biology at college and was working down in Florida on some conservation program. Then her grandma died, left her a bed-and-breakfast in Fort Peck, Montana, and she's gone back there to run it."

"A bit of a career change," Raoul said. "Does she plan to stay there or sell up?"

"Not so big a change. She grew up there and loves the place. It's right on a lake, lots of marine life and conservation stuff for her to involve herself with. The bed-and-breakfast is a bit run-down, but she plans to renovate the place and attract summer tourists. Hiking, fishing, stuff like that. Tourism is making a big contribution to the Montana economy nowadays."

"Sounds like a plan," Raoul said. "So what's the problem?"

"Far as she's concerned, nothing at all. Every time I email her, she tells me everything's just dandy. But I keep in contact with a couple of old guys in Fort Peck. We go way back, and they've kinda taken it upon themselves to look out for Briana. Seems someone doesn't want her to succeed with her little B and B and is actively sabotaging her efforts."

"In what respect?" Raoul asked.

"That's just the problem, I don't know much more than that. Briana is as tight-lipped with my buddies as she is with me, which makes me wonder if I'm blowing this up out of all proportion. Still, for my own peace of mind, I wondered if you had anyone who could stop by and check up on her for me."

Raoul and Zeke exchanged a glance. The woman was twenty-four and had told her dad she didn't need any help. Raoul also knew that the major wasn't one to panic and that he must be pretty steamed up to even ask for help. Raoul and Zeke had served with him and respected his judgment.

"Sure, we can do that. Is she open for business yet?" Raoul asked.

"I don't think so. Does it matter?"

"Well, I'm guessing she won't like it if my guys turn up and make it obvious you've sent them."

"Ah, I see what you mean. Good thinking."

"Leave it with us, Major. We'll send someone over for a weekend's hunting and fishing and see what shakes loose."

"I appreciate it, Raoul."

"No problem." Raoul cut the connection and looked at Zeke. "Who do we have in Montana?" he asked.

"We've got Fergal, Harley, and Gus in Columbia Falls. They won't have much to do this time of year."

"Not much call for ski instructors in the summer." Raoul flicked through his phonebook, found Fergal's number and called him up. "Hey, buddy," he said when Fergal answered, "how do you guys fancy a weekend's fishing?"

Chapter Two

Briana clenched her fists, dug the ragged fingernails into her palms severely enough to make her eyes water, and counted to ten in her head.

"I don't care what it says on your inventory," she told the person on the other end of the phone, resisting the temptation to grind her jaw. "I didn't order roof tiles. I ordered roof timbers. Big difference."

She listened, wondering if steam was actually coming out of her ears as the kid she was talking to trotted out the usual platitudes.

Give me strength. "Yes, I agree someone's made a mistake, but it isn't me. Now I've got a whole pallet load of roof tiles stuck right outside my door, obstructing my entrance, and workmen due to arrive tomorrow to fix the timber that you haven't supplied. What are you going to do about it?"

Briana was put on hold while her call was passed up the line. She figured that was just as well. The child who'd answered was worse than useless. Briana needed someone to yell at, but she drew the line at tearing the office junior a new one. The way she felt right now, she'd probably traumatize him for life if she let rip with the profanities buzzing around her over-stretched brain.

Five minutes later she'd been told that the tiles couldn't be collected until Monday and the timber wouldn't be delivered until then, either. Monday! Today was Thursday. She couldn't wait that long. Arguing, threatening, and cajoling got her nowhere. Fuck it, this was more than just bad luck! Everything she tried to do here seemed to go wrong, and she was beginning to think someone had it in for her.

Briana disconnected, sat down on a packing case, and expelled several deep, calming breaths. All she wanted to do was restore the lodge where she'd spent most of her childhood to its former glory and open it up as a bed-and-breakfast. They made it look so easy on those makeover television shows. She had all the necessary permissions, subject to completion of the work and compliance with a million safety regulations. But if she couldn't even get the damned roof repaired, she'd have failed at the first hurdle and would be left with no choice but to sell up.

"Ain't gonna happen," she told her motley collection of animals, all rescues.

Bradley and Boris, the two kittens she'd saved from being drowned, were chasing a ball of string across the floor and took not a blind bit of notice. Max, the nondescript mongrel who'd been with her since she graduated college, picked up on her mood and shoved his shaggy head beneath her hand, glancing up at her through mournful eyes.

"Don't take any notice of me," she said to him. "I just need a moment to regroup, then we'll decide what to do."

Apparently satisfied that she wasn't going into meltdown, Max trotted outside, and Briana returned to her cogitations. Her dad kept emailing, almost as though he sensed things weren't going right for her. She hadn't told him anything about her problems. That was partly because she didn't want to be branded a failure, but also because he had enough to worry about, being stationed in Iraq. Besides, she'd seen so little of her dad during her childhood years that she'd never gotten into the habit of confiding in him. It was her grandma who had been her mother and father all rolled into one, as well as confidant and best friend.

Briana dashed impatiently at the tears forming in her eyes. She *never* cried as a general rule, but whenever she thought about Gran she didn't seem able to stop. Damn it, why did she have to die so young? And why hadn't Briana been here? As though summoned back from the grave by the sheer force of her will, Briana sensed Gran's calming presence, giving her the strength she needed to rise above this latest calamity.

Briana had set herself a year to get the place up and running, ready for next year's summer trade. If she was careful with her funds and managed to sell a few of her photographs, she ought to be able to survive until then. The winters she'd have to herself for photography and the conservations programs she was so passionate about. Not many people came to Montana for outdoor activities in the winter—especially not to such isolated places as hers. Not that Briana looked upon it as being isolated. She loved every inch of the place, always had and always would. The only other option was to sell up, and that was unthinkable.

"Hey, anyone home?"

Shit! Greg Stone was here. Again. Briana blew her nose and dabbed at her eyes, managing to pull herself together moments before her old flame walked into the room.

"Hey, Briana, how's it going?"

As always, he was dressed to assassinate. Anyone wearing a suit in this rural location looked out of place, but Greg had the good looks and the confidence to carry it off. What's more, he appeared to know it.

"Hi, Greg. What brings you out this way?"

"I had business in town, so I figured I'd make a quick detour and see how things were going."

Briana didn't believe him. He worked out of Glasgow, which was nineteen miles drive from Fort Peck. She was five miles the other side of town. Arborfield Lodge was only accessible on very narrow roads—not much more than dirt tracks in places. For Briana, the inaccessibility of the place only added to its charm, unless she needed supplies delivered, of course. She glanced out the door at Greg's brand-new SUV, now splattered in mud, which reinforced her suspicions about her college sweetheart's impromptu visit.

"It's slow going, but I'll get there."

When Greg gave her body a quick once-over, Briana tried to see herself through his eyes. Plaster was splattered all over her clothes, and probably over her face, too. Talk about chalk and cheese. She flipped her long, red braid over her shoulder and withstood his scrutiny without blinking. Was he expecting her to offer him tea or something?

"I didn't know you were replacing the roof tiles," he said, glancing at the unwelcome and inconveniently located pallet.

"I'm not. There was a mix-up."

"Oh. Sorry about that." But he didn't look the slightest bit sorry.

"Yeah, well, shit happens."

"I thought you said Ben and Joe were going to fix your roof timbers for you this weekend on their own time."

"Obviously, I shall have to rearrange." She turned back to the wall she'd been fixing and pointedly picked up her plaster tray. "Now, you'll have to excuse me. I don't want to have to mix up more plaster, and it'll dry out if I'm not careful."

"Sure, babe." But he still lingered. "Actually, I wondered if you were free for dinner. I haven't seen a lot of you since you got back."

"Sorry, Greg. I'm gonna have to take a rain check."

He didn't look pleased, which again made Briana wonder why he was being so persistent. He could have just about any woman he wanted, and, from what her gran had told her when she was still alive, he'd spread his favors liberally around the local female population— married or otherwise. Why he was so intent upon pursuing her, she couldn't have said. They'd gotten along fine in school, but she was a very different person now and couldn't see that they had anything in common. He certainly didn't light her fire.

"All work and no play—"

Max reappeared and a threating growl rumbled in his throat when he saw Greg. Briana didn't understand it. Max was the friendliest dog on God's earth, but for some inexplicable reason he'd taken a dislike to Greg. The feeling appeared to be mutual, and Greg backed a hasty retreat toward his car.

"I'll give you a call," he said. "And next time I won't take *no* for an answer. If there's anything I can do to help you in the meantime, just say the word."

"Thanks, Greg, I might just do that."

But she wouldn't. She had no idea why she was rejecting his frequent offers of assistance. Sometimes she was too independent for her own good. With a deep sigh, Briana returned to her plastering.

* * * *

"You sure this is the place?" Fergal asked from behind the wheel of his truck. "Seems pretty remote."

"It's the place," Harley replied from the passenger seat, where he had a map of the area stretched across his lap.

"You could switch the GPS on," said Gus's voice from the backseat.

"Thought you were asleep," Harley said, glancing over his shoulder at Gus's prostrate body and catching his lazy smile.

"What, with you two gabbing away like old women?" He expelled a long-suffering sigh. "Call yourselves *elite* forces. You guys couldn't navigate your way out of a paper bag."

"Shut the fuck up," Fergal said amiably, shooting Gus the finger. "I think this is the turning. Shit!" Fergal swerved to avoid an SUV coming at speed from the opposite direction. The driver leaned on his horn, forcing Fergal to pull over into a ravine. "Holy fuck, who does that guy think he is?"

The other driver slowed to take a good look at Fergal and Harley. Gus didn't even bother to sit up to see what the fuss was about. Fergal lowered his window, ready to tear the guy off a strip, but he gunned his engine and disappeared in a spray of gravel and exhaust smoke.

Fergal drove on for another mile, enjoying the serenity of the countryside in late spring. He noticed wildflowers growing along the verge, and the only sound, apart from the noise of their engine, was that of birds' mating calls. Then they turned another corner and were looking right down at the lake. The water shimmered beneath the afternoon sun, a dozen different shades of turquoise reflected in its torpid surface, and he could see wading birds paddling about in the shallows.

"That's quite a view," Harley said. "Almost worth the uncomfortable ride."

"I'll say," Fergal agreed, pulling over and cutting the engine. "Apparently it's the fifth largest artificial lake in the States."

"What's happening?" Gus sat up and pressed his face to the window. "Shit, that's real tranquil. Must be some pretty good fishing to be had."

"I read up on it," Harley said. "They got walleye, pike, Chinook salmon, and pallid sturgeons, and a whole load of other marine life swimming about down there."

"A good place for our client to start a B and B, what with her place being away from the town," Fergal said, restarting the engine. "People can come here to commune with nature and all that shit."

They followed the dirt track skirting the lake for another half mile and came to a side turning with a handmade sign advertising *Arborfield Lodge*.

"That's us," Fergal said, turning into the unmade drive that made the track they'd just been on seem like a major highway by comparison. "Shit, these potholes would rip out the exhaust on an ordinary car."

"No one has ordinary cars out here," Gus replied.

The driveway led them to what was obviously the back of a log cabin. A very large log cabin that looked as if it had been there for a long time. It had definitely seen better days. They followed the driveway around to the front of the horseshoe-shaped building, one wing of which had its roof covered with tarpaulins.

"I like it," Fergal said.

"Me, too." Harley and Fergal turn to look at Gus askance. He made it a rule never to agree with anything either of them said. "Hey, I'm not a complete moron. I can see through all the work that needs to be done. This place will be real cool once it's fixed up."

There was a pallet of what appeared to be roofing slates right outside the door to the lodge. Fergal pulled up alongside it and cut the engine. The lake was real close, just a hundred yards or so in front of the lodge, down a gentle incline. There was a weathered dock that presumably belonged to the lodge but no boats attached to it. A scruffy dog came loping up to them, barking its head off and wagging its tail in lopsided circles.

"Hey, fella, what's up?" Fergal scratched his ears. "You the only person home?"

"Nope, I'm here."

They all looked in the direction of the voice that came from the front door of the lodge. A tall woman with bright-red hair in a long braid and with plaster all over her clothing and face stood in the doorway with her hands on her hips. And what hips they were, too. The rest of her wasn't too shabby, either. Just as Gus could see through the work that needed to be done to the lodge, so Fergal could see through the woman's loose clothing to all the enticing curves beneath it. She had deep-green eyes, a cute turned-up nose, and delicate features that complimented one another, freckles and plaster splatters notwithstanding.

Something stirred deep inside Fergal as they traded glances—something more profound than mere lust or attraction—something that had lain dormant for way too long.

"Something I can do for you gentlemen?" she asked.

Chapter Three

"Now what?"

Briana was pissed when she heard an engine approaching, figuring it had to be Greg returning to try and change her mind about dinner. She was so far off the beaten track that no one came here by accident. What was it about Greg anyway? Hadn't he heard of telephones? She didn't want to be bad friends with him, but she could do without the interruption. She could pretend to be out, she supposed, but he'd know she wasn't because her car was outside. With an irritated sigh, she put down her plaster tray and went to the front door.

What she saw there stopped her dead in her tracks. Three strangers had just climbed out of a truck and were focusing devastating smiles on her. The sight of all that masculine vitality— bulging muscles and hard, taut bodies—sent her stomach into free fall and, goddamn it, made her juices flow. It had been a while.

She moistened her lips and tried to speak, but her voice sounded like Minnie Mouse on steroids. She cleared her throat and tried again.

"Are you lost?" she asked.

"We heard there was a B and B someplace around here," one guy answered. "We're looking for a weekend's fishing."

"You're a year too early," she replied. *Please come back when I'm open.*

"Oh, that's okay," said the second guy. "We don't mind roughing it."

"I'm sorry, but…"

Briana's words trailed off, and a fulminating anger kicked aside the lustful thoughts that had slipped past her guard. These guys hadn't come upon her place by chance. No way! Besides, how would strangers know she was thinking of opening a B and B sometime before she died of old age? They'd been sent here by someone to check up on her, and it didn't take a rocket scientist to figure out who that someone had to be. Despite their casual clothes and long hair, the way they moved with precision and authority like a well-oiled machine screamed of the military.

"My father sent you," she said through tightly gritted teeth.

"Busted!" the third guy said with a killer grin. "You must be Briana."

"And you gentlemen must be leaving." She folded her arms beneath her breasts and glowered at them. "I don't know why my dad thought I needed anyone to hold my hand, but I can assure you I don't."

The first guy stepped forward, and she expected him to argue the toss. Given the state of the place when seen through a stranger's eyes, she couldn't altogether blame him if he did. Even so, she'd give him a piece of her mind if he dared to try it.

He didn't.

Instead he stuck out a large hand, and she instinctively took it. As soon as his long fingers curled around her palm, she regretted doing so. A disturbing thrill jolted her body as the warmth from his hand transferred itself to her entire body, creating a bewildering paradox of pleasure and longing to thrump deep within her core.

"I'm Fergal Stanton," he said, still trapping her hand inside his. "This here is Harley Osborne." The guy with light-brown hair and turquoise eyes waved to her. "And last but not least we have Gus Dalton."

"Hey there," Gus said, his dark-blond hair lifting in the breeze, soft gray eyes sparkling with something she couldn't quite identify as they regarded her. "Nice meeting you."

Briana snatched her hand back. "Nice meeting you all as well, but as you can see, I don't have anywhere to put guests right now. So, if you'll excuse me—"

"I have a suggestion to make," Fergal said. "Your daddy's real worried about you, and he sent us to check you're all right."

"Well, you've seen me and you can tell him that I'm just peachy."

"No, you're not," Fergal said softly.

"Who the hell?" How could they possibly know things weren't going as planned? "Ah, now I get it. Seth and Maurice. I might have known."

"Who?" Harley asked.

"Two old guys who live in town. They were friends of my grandmother's." Briana tried not to smile but couldn't hold it in. "Every day in the summer, they're to be found at a table outside the barber shop, drinking coffee and shooting the breeze. In the winter they transfer inside the shop and it's more of the same. Nothing, and I mean nothing, happens in this valley that they don't get to hear about. Dad must be in touch with them. Hmm, I shall have words to say to those two interfering—"

"Isn't it nice to have people who care about you?" Gus asked.

"Caring is one thing. Interfering is something else."

"Why don't we come in, visit for a while, and then, if you still want us to leave, we'll go." Fergal shrugged. "Thing is, we have to report back to our boss and tell him everything's okay, so he can reassure your old man. Wouldn't be doing our job right if we didn't at least go that far."

"And who's going to finish plastering my wall while we waste time talking?"

"We will," Harley and Gus said together.

"That's not what I meant," she replied hastily. It would mean they'd have to stay. The lodge was large, but it wasn't big enough for the three of them *and* her to cohabit without them invading her personal space. Besides, accepting their help would be a sign of weakness. "I don't need your help."

"These roof tiles aren't in the right place," Fergal said, kicking at the pallet with a worn work boot. "You should have made them leave 'em closer to where they're needed."

"They aren't needed at all," she said before she could stop herself.

"Why not?" the three of them asked together.

"You have a bare roof," Fergal added alone, glancing up at the wing with the tarpaulin. "Presumably that's where they need to be."

Oh shit, they really weren't going to leave unless she came clean. Her anger intensified since she was aware her dad hadn't sent them because he was worried about her. He would go to any lengths just to be able to say that he'd told her so. Her father enjoyed giving orders, but insubordination didn't sit easily with him.

"Okay, come inside," she said with a heavy sigh. "We'll discuss my *welfare* and then you can leave. Deal?"

"Sure," Fergal said lazily.

The great room had always seemed enormous to Briana and seemed especially so now that she was painstakingly repairing every inch of the walls. Invaded by three large bodies, it now felt crowded, the atmosphere strained yet weirdly anticipatory.

Get a grip!

Briana examined her visitors as they examined the room. All three of them wore faded denim jeans that sat low on their hips and showcased trim asses. Their T-shirts were poor disguises for their broad shoulders, heavily muscled chests, and tapering waists. They joshed with one another in a way that suggested the sort of close friendship Briana had never known, causing her to feel a spike of envy.

Presumably they weren't still in the military, but they obviously kept themselves in shape. They stood with legs slightly apart, relaxed and easy, and yet their stances conveyed power, strength, and integrity. It was impossible to ignore their animal vitality, but she'd give it her best shot. She absolutely didn't want them here, but already felt safer because they were. That realization brought her up short. Since when had she felt unsafe, or lonely for that matter?

"Nice room," Fergal said, his eyes focused on the enormous brick fireplace. "It must be real cozy in the winter with a fire roaring up the chimney and the drapes closed against the winter weather."

"What drapes?" she replied, deadpan.

"I've got a good imagination, honey. I can see through works in progress to the treasures hidden beneath." But his rich gaze was now focused on her shabby work clothes rather than the room itself.

"Well, give the man a prize." Briana was furious because she felt herself blushing and could see he was amused to have gotten a reaction from her. *Bastard!*

"When do you plan to open?" Gus asked.

"Spring next year, if I can get it all together in time."

Harley smiled at her. "What's likely to stop you?"

She shrugged. "Everything's taking longer than I imagined."

"How many people you got working with you?" Fergal asked, looking around like he expected a gaggle of workmen to appear from nowhere.

"I'm doing as much as I can myself," she replied evasively.

Fergal flexed a brow. "You can tile roofs?"

"I've got a couple of guys coming to do that for me at weekends. Same with the electric and plumbing."

"Working off the clock? You haven't employed licensed contractors?"

"Right. The people helping me knew my grandmother. I pay them cash. It's the only way I can afford to get things done."

"So, what happened with the roof tiles?" Fergal asked, settling one buttock on the edge of a packing case, looking like he was settling in for a long stay.

"You're really not going to leave until I tell you everything, are you?" She glowered at him. "You just wait until I get my hands on Seth and Maurice."

"Look at it from your dad's point of view. He's stuck out there in Iraq and gets emails saying his little girl's having problems. It's a dad's job to protect his child, no matter how grown up she is," Fergal said, undressing her with his eyes and smirking.

Briana hated it when men did that. A great believer in fighting fire with fire, she returned the favor, running her eyes slowly down the length of his tall frame. Slightly wavy brown hair almost reached his shoulders, and deep-brown eyes burned with an unholy light as he watched her watching him. The day's growth of stubble on his strong jaw suited him, adding to his rugged allure, but hell would freeze over before Briana admitted it.

Her gaze skimmed over his sculpted chest and landed on the faded denim surrounding his zipper. The bulge was impressive, and she was filled with a reckless desire to find out what he was packing. Was it her imagination or did the bulge swell beneath her scrutiny? She was conscious of the atmosphere between them, warm, taut, and expectant. So, too, it seemed, was Fergal because it was him who broke the loaded silence.

"It's what dads do," he said with a mock smile.

"I beg your pardon?" Briana snatched her gaze away from his cock and moistened her lips with the tip of her tongue.

"It's a father's job to worry about his child, even when that child's an adult and doesn't want to be worried about."

She curled her upper lip. "Mine obviously didn't get the memo."

"Perhaps he's trying to make up for lost time," Harley said. "He's a career soldier, so you probably don't need me to tell you that family life and soldiering don't always mix."

"I'd expect you guys to make excuses for him."

"Honey, we're just telling it like it is," Gus said. "It doesn't make your dad right. All we're saying is, we know it's not easy to juggle the two."

"Tell us about it," Fergal invited.

She glanced at him. Yep, the bulge had subsided. Briana felt ridiculously pleased to have given him an erection, just by looking at him. *Take that!* It seemed only fair. Since inviting them inside and being in close proximity to all those rippling muscles and free-flowing testosterone, her honey had been trickling freely, soaking her panties, and her nipples were conducting a full-scale war against the fabric of her bra. Geez!

"It's a long story," she belatedly replied to Fergal's question.

Gus disappeared into the kitchen and starting playing with the coffeemaker. Ha, good luck with that. The machine was older than she was, an antique in the annals of electronic gadgets. It was still in perfect working order, *if* you knew how to work it. It also happened to make the best coffee she'd ever tasted, but she didn't count on getting a cup any time soon unless she offered to help. And that she had no intention of doing.

Annoyingly, Gus appeared to figure it out for himself. She heard him humming as he moved about the kitchen, ground the beans, and assembled the stuff he needed. He opened and closed the old cabinets and in no time at all he reappeared with a tray loaded with a full coffeepot, cream, and sugar. He'd even unearthed her emergency stash of chocolate chip cookies.

"We've got all day, honey," Gus said, plonking himself down next to her and pouring her a mug of steaming coffee. "Tell us what we can do to help."

"Helping ladies in distress is our specialty," Harley added.

I'll just bet it is.

* * * *

Fergal watched her blow on the surface of her coffee, cradling the mug in both of her hands as she stalled for time. She clearly *was* in trouble here, that much was immediately obvious. She'd taken on a huge project and seemed to think she could handle it alone. Fergal wasn't sexist. He could see she'd done a good job of replastering one of the walls in this room, and she'd probably be equally good at painting those walls. But they were cosmetic jobs. The real work—the roof, electrics, and plumbing—were skilled jobs that she seemed to think she could farm out on an ad-hoc basis. It would never work, and he suspected she already knew it. He also suspected that she was too proud to admit it, or to ask for help.

"What branch of the service were you guys in?" she asked.

Fergal had figured she'd ask something to deflect attention away from herself and was happy enough to answer her.

"Three fine upstanding former Special Operations Command Marines at your service, ma'am," he said.

She trapped a smile. "Always faithful, always forward," she muttered. "The silent warriors."

Gus elevated a brow. "The lady knows our motto *and* our nickname."

"I'm an army brat, but don't expect me to tell you I'm impressed because you made the grade in that elite corp."

"Wouldn't think of it," Harley said, sending her a wink.

"Let me guess," she said. "You have to ace courses in physical fitness, swimming, and hand-to-hand combat, just to get through the initial selection course."

Fergal nodded. "Something like that."

She didn't need to know about the rifle and pistol marksmanship, irregular warfare operations or the requirement to be an advanced linguist. She had a rough idea of their capabilities, which was a start. All they had to do now was to build on that and persuade her to trust them. She'd assured them she was okay, so technically they'd done what they were sent here to do. Fergal could see for himself that she *was* fit—very fit. She was also as feisty as heck, but walking away from her simply wasn't an option. She was in urgent need of their help, whether she realized it or not. He didn't need to ask his buddies if they felt the same way. He knew they did. They were as taken with her as Fergal was and would go that extra mile for her for no other reason than making her smile.

Fergal knew, just from making occasional eye contact with Harley and Gus, that their thoughts were already veering in the same direction as his. It was a while since they'd found a woman they all wanted to share. Briana fit their exacting requirements, and then some. All that red hair and freckles. That stacked body and endlessly long legs. She only had to look at him and he hardened. When had that last happened? Shit, when she gave him the once-over, he'd almost shot his load in his pants. How embarrassing would that have been? Fergal, the master of control, losing it because a cute chick gave him the eye. His buds would laugh themselves silly.

He longed to loosen her braid and help her out of those dirty clothes. He wanted to see her hair billowing down her back and her body as nature intended. Problem was, no way would he try to persuade her to play with them until they'd figured out what was going on around her. If she came to them, it had to be of her own free will, and not because she felt she owed them some sort of debt.

Shit, having an honorable streak sometimes sucked.

"Have things been going wrong here?" Harley asked. "I don't mean to imply you're not doing a good job, honey, but it's one hell of a project to tackle alone."

Fergal could see that she'd been about to tear Harley a new one for implying she couldn't cope. His hastily worded explanation appeared to satisfy her, and she shared a grimace between them.

"Yeah, I guess the road to satisfying all the trillions of safety requirements is rougher than I'd thought. Sometimes I'm tempted just to tart the place up and live in it alone. That would be much easier, but unfortunately wouldn't provide me with an income."

"You could sell," Gus suggested.

"Not a chance! I was brought up in this house and love it like crazy. I'll find a way to hang on to it, no matter what I have to do."

"What happened to your mom?" Harley asked.

She shrugged. "Mom and Dad married right out of college. They were way too young to make such a big commitment, and, like you said earlier, Mom couldn't adapt to army life. I don't remember much about her. She took off with a stockbroker when I was little, and I've had no contact with her since."

"Ouch!" Fergal sent her a sympathetic smile. "She's never tried to contact you?"

Briana shook her head. "Nope."

"That must have been tough."

"What you've never had you don't miss. I wouldn't know her if I ran into her in the street." *Because I destroyed all the pictures Dad had of her as soon as I was old enough to realize how little I must have meant to her.* "Dad brought me here to live with Gran and was an infrequent visitor, in between postings."

"He didn't take you along?" Harley flapped a hand. "Stupid question. He couldn't, not without his wife being with him."

"Right." She fiddled with the hem of her shirt, so not wanting to talk about this stuff. "Gran more than made up for his absences. I adored her. We shared everything, and I didn't need anyone else."

Fergal nodded, like he thought he understood. A tough guy like him couldn't possibly, but, meeting his gaze and seeing a flicker of recognition flash through his eyes, somehow she knew that he did. She wasn't the only wounded soldier on parade, but she suspected the ice cap would melt before Fergal admitted to his emotional weaknesses.

"Now Gran's gone, too, and I need to move on," she said briskly.

"It's too late for your dad to be part of your life?" Fergal asked.

"I don't need him. I don't need anyone." Briana jutted her chin and shared a glance between the three of them. "And, grateful though I am for your visit, that includes all of you as well, gentlemen."

Chapter Four

"Ain't gonna happen until we've satisfied ourselves you're okay," Fergal said with an easy smile.

"I could throw you out."

He laughed. "You're certainly welcome to try."

"Don't imagine that I couldn't do it, tough guy. Just because there're three of you, doesn't mean you have the upper hand." She shared a sweetly sarcastic smile between them. "Just so you know, I'm a natural redhead, with the temper to match. It's not my fault. It's embedded in my DNA. I don't freak at the sight of blood *and* I don't fight fair."

Gus chuckled. "Do you have any idea how gorgeous you look when you get mad?"

"Oh, for goodness sake!" She threw up her hands. "If I tell you what's been going on, then will you leave?"

"Depends upon what you tell us," Harley replied.

Briana sipped at her coffee, waiting for her temper to subside as she tried to decide how much to tell them. Unlike some of the locals, their expressions conveyed respect rather than condescension at what she, a mere female, was attempting to achieve. Even so, she absolutely didn't need to share—not with them, certainly not with Greg—but something about their genuine-seeming concern decided her. Not that there was anything they could do. They seemed to think there was some grand scheme put in place by faceless entities to make her fail. Briana knew better. There was no conspiracy. Her problems were simply attributable to bad luck. If she could make them understand that, presumably they'd leave her in peace.

"Before I say anything, I need you to promise that you won't pass it on to my dad," she said, addressing the comment to Fergal, who appeared to be the leader of this trio. "You were sent to make sure I'm okay, which, as you can see, I am. I don't want him getting involved here. Not that he can physically do so when he's overseas, but your presence here shows that his tentacles reach far. I don't need him on my case. It's way too late for that."

"Agreed," Fergal said without hesitation. "Why not give us a guided tour and tell us what's gone wrong along the way?"

"Fair enough." Briana put her coffee mug aside and stood up. "Follow me, guys."

She led them into the west wing, conscious of three pairs of eyes following her ass. She was tempted to wiggle it, aware that she had nothing to be ashamed of, at least in the backside department. Briana resisted, figuring it was better not to let them think she had any personal interest in them even if, on a visceral level at least, she absolutely did. She'd defy any woman with a libido and a pulse to react to them any other way. She'd have to be blind not to be affected by such a plethora of masculine vitality crowding her out, messing with her head, sending spikes of lust jolting through her whenever one of them fixed her with a slow, predatory smile that suggested its owner liked what he saw. Briana glanced down at the state of her clothing and grimaced. *Yeah, right!*

"This part of the house has six bedrooms in various stages of decoration, each with the beginnings of an en-suite bathroom springing into life. I've had to sacrifice a room on each side of the corridor to make space for the bathrooms," she said. "I'm told that even out here in the wilds, people expect their own facilities."

"There were eight bedrooms to start with and two bathrooms," Gus said, sounding surprised. "What did your grandparents use this place for?"

"Same thing I want to, except in their day they didn't have to abide by all the regulations that are holding me up." She smiled, pointing to a faded sepia picture on one of the walls, showing men from another age sitting on the dock, fishing. "That's my granddad, and some of his buddies from out of town, taken more than fifty years ago."

"Time's kinda stood still around these parts," Gus said, examining the picture. "If that's one of the reasons why you love the place then I totally get where you're coming from. Life moves on way too quick nowadays."

"Yeah, it's so quiet out here that it gets under your skin after a while. There's lots of activity on this lake, but not on this side of it. We're too inaccessible, which is just the way I want it to stay. It gives the lodge a unique edge that I plan to trade on to attract customers."

"How come the work on the bathrooms has stopped?" Fergal asked, poking his head through one of the door openings.

Briana wrinkled her nose. "The guys doing the plumbing got sent off on an out of state job by their employers."

Fergal flexed his brows. "Is that normal?"

"No, they were pretty surprised when they got the job, as a matter of fact. It's never happened before, apparently, but in these difficult times economically their employer had to cast his net wider. When he got the contract the guys had no choice but to go."

"That must have messed up your schedule," Harley said.

"Yeah, on top of one of the electricians having an accident that's kept him off work for over a week, it didn't help any. And don't get me started on the building inspectors." Briana puffed air through her lips. "They seem to be here all the time, poking around, finding more and more things for me to comply with."

"Presumably you didn't need to apply for change of use, seeing as how the building has been used to accommodate visitors for years," Fergal said.

"That's what I thought, but it seems I was wrong. I had to get an engineer to do a professional evaluation, which cost a small fortune, permission from the local planning council, and...well, you wouldn't believe me if I told you about all the other hoops I've had to jump through just to carry on where Gran left off."

"I assume she never bothered to get approval and no one worried her over it."

"Right, but they're sure as hell worrying me. Seems I can't do anything right first time, even though I do precisely what they ask me to."

Fergal frowned. "It's either bureaucracy at its finest or someone's got it in for you." He placed a hand on the small of her back and guided her out of the half-completed bathroom. "Seems your dad was right to be concerned."

"There's absolutely no reason why anyone would try to sabotage my efforts." Briana shook off his hand. It felt too damned good resting there, and she couldn't afford to lean on it or him. "Don't see shadows where none exist. The only enemy I'm fighting is, as you just pointed out, bureaucracy."

"Who was the guy in the SUV who passed us down the road?" Gus asked. "He must have been coming from here."

"And drove us off the road," Harley added, scowling.

"Oh God, that would have been Greg. He came up to see if I was okay. He's always running late for some appointment or other and drives way too fast even when he isn't."

"Who's Greg?" Fergal and Harley asked together.

"An old friend."

Fergal shot her a look. "Friend or flame?"

"None of your damned business."

"It is when he tried to run us off the road," Fergal responded. "No, he *did* run us off the road. Deliberately, I'm sure."

"He wouldn't do that."

"You're pretty keen to defend him, but you weren't there, so you can't possibly know what happened."

"Okay," she said huffily. "If you must know, Greg and I were an item during our last couple of years at college. He wanted to get married as soon as we graduated, I didn't, so we went our separate ways. End of story."

Fergal scowled. "So it ended badly, but now you're buddies again?"

"He got over it, realized I was right, and married someone else. It didn't work out and they divorced a year ago."

"What does he do?" Harley asked.

"He works with his father. He has a marketing business in Glasgow."

Gus, who appeared to have taken a dislike to Greg, screwed up his features and grunted. "What does he market?"

"I'm not sure." Briana shrugged. "I think he helps local people to get the right exposure for their businesses, stuff like that."

"And this Greg drives all the way out here, just to see if you're all right?" Fergal fixed her with a questioning glance. "Seems a bit extreme."

"Perhaps, but that's just the way he is." Briana wasn't about to tell them that she agreed with that assessment. She'd never get rid of them if she did. *Tell them!* "Come on, I'll show you the rest."

They moved back into the great room. Its furniture was covered in dust sheets, the walls were stripped bare, the windows grimy. It must look cold and uninviting to strangers, but Briana didn't see it that way. For her it held a cornucopia of memories from happier times— an atmosphere she was determined to recreate.

"This is the hub of the house, where guests will be able to relax, exaggerate about their day's fishing, make new friends, and generally de-stress."

Fergal bent to scratch Max's ears. "I can feel the atmosphere, even as the room is now. It's a fabulous setting and a room with positive vibes. Your plan ought to work."

She rolled her eyes. "If I ever satisfy the inspectors."

"I can't imagine you ever leaving anyone unsatisfied, darlin'," Harley said.

"Stop flirting with me, Mr. Osborne," Briana replied, sending him a quelling glance. "I'm serious about this, and I don't appreciate being patronized."

"Hey, I was deadly serious, and I certainly wasn't patronizing you."

"Quit fooling," Gus said, shooting Harley the finger. Briana smiled in spite of herself but quickly straightened her lips out again. They were trying to charm her, and she was in no mood to be charmed. They might have gotten her juices flowing, but Briana didn't do casual sex. She couldn't remember the last time she'd done any sort of sex, other than the self-induced variety, but that was beside the point.

One of the kittens fell into the room and tried to climb up Harley's leg. Harley laughed as he picked Boris up and tickled his chin. The kitten was swamped between Harley's large hands, just the tips of his ears and a pair of huge eyes visible. Briana could see that he was being real gentle, helping to redeem him for his earlier flippancy in her eyes. Anyone who cared about her waifs and strays couldn't be all bad.

"Cute kittens," he said.

"I think so, although they do tend to complicate things. I can't seem to get through to them that electrical wires are not to be chased or chewed and holes in walls aren't knocked through just so they can hide behind them."

The guys all laughed as they followed her through to the kitchen.

"This was always my favorite part of the house," she said. "Gran spent half her life in here baking, and I love these old cabinets. I'm going to have them stripped back to the original maple and then varnished. They're too good to scrap."

"I agree," Gus said. "They don't make roomy larders like this one anymore."

"Right. For years Gran didn't have a fridge. She just used the cold marble shelf in the larder to keep things cool."

Fergal nodded. "That would work in this climate."

He focused brown eyes gleaming with unsettling intelligence upon her, causing havoc with her equilibrium. She was furious when the sexual magnetism that seemed to cling to him blasted shards of pleasure through her entire body. She was pathetic! All women presumably responded to their toxic charm in the same way. Well, sorry, guys, Briana thought, but I don't have time for all that nonsense. Wilting at their feet like some sort of lovelorn heroine in a cheap novel couldn't be fitted into her tight schedule this week.

"Now I'm going to have to get all sorts of expensive modern devices in here to satisfy the inspectors," she said briskly, turning away from Fergal but regretting it when her gaze clashed with Harley's. He winked at her, like he could interpret her thoughts, and her face flooded with color. Again. "I absolutely refuse to part with the cabinets," she said, walking out of the kitchen.

She led them through to the formal dining room which was dominated by an old maple table that could comfortably accommodate twenty people.

"Great table," Gus said, running his hand across the wood.

"It's been here forever, and it's where I plan to feed my guests. There won't be lots of prissy little tables, just old faithful here." She patted the scarred wood with genuine affection. "People can eat together or starve."

"Sounds like a plan." Fergal laughed at her passion as he glanced around the room, his gaze falling upon a series of framed photographs on the wall. He walked up to take a closer look. "Say, these are good. Who took them?"

"I did. Photography's a hobby of mine."

"You're good enough to be a professional," Gus said, examining a shot she'd taken of a manatee and its baby. "You took these during your conservation program in Florida, presumably."

"Thanks, and yes, I did. That's what I'll do here in the winter, when there are no guests. Get involved with conservation and take pictures. I've managed to sell a few to magazines already. Hopefully I can shift a few more when I get time, to help defray some of the costs being eaten up by this project."

"You could display some on the walls here," Harley suggested. "Put price tags on them and sell them to your visitors. Or, come to that, you could take pictures of the visitors themselves. Tourists love all that shit."

Briana blinked. "That's a good idea. Why didn't I think of that?"

Harley laughed. "I know I'm brilliant. There's no need to thank me."

She shot him a look. "I wasn't going to. I still haven't forgiven you for earlier."

"You have to ignore Harley," Fergal said. "We do. He's a fool, but we kinda love him anyway."

"Well, just so long as I don't have to love him, too."

"We wouldn't inflict that sort of torture on you, sweetheart," Gus assured her.

"Is this where you live?" Fergal asked, opening a door on the far side of the dining room.

"Don't go in there!"

Too late. All three of them piled through the door to Gran's private domain like they had every right in the world to intrude.

"Sorry," Fergal said, backing out again. "I can see you haven't touched that part of the house yet."

"It was Gran's sitting room, bedroom, and bathroom, and…well, I can't bring myself to clear it out yet."

"So you must be sleeping in one of the rooms we didn't go into in the other wing?" Gus said.

"Yes. Besides, this part of this wing doesn't have a roof."

"The new tiles?" Harley said.

"No, the old slates are in great order. I'll show you." She led them outside through a side door and pointed to the slates that had been removed from the roof and piled up outside a shed. "They made stuff to last in those days. The modern ones aren't nearly as good. The problem is that my surveyor found woodworm in the wooden trusses in this part of the roof, so the slates had to be stripped off so the beams can be replaced. That was what was supposed to be delivered today, but instead they sent me a whole pallet of tiles that I didn't order." Briana expelled a frustrated sigh. "They can't deliver the timber I need until next week, which means I'll have nothing for the guys to do when they turn up Saturday."

"If they fucked the order up," Fergal said, "they'll have to put it right."

"That's what I tried to tell them, but they're having none of it. This remote location works against me sometimes. They only come out this way with a particular truck that can handle the road on certain days of the week. Right now that truck is elsewhere, and they won't call it back to correct their mistake."

"Where does the timber come from?" Fergal asked.

"A builders' merchant on the other side of Glasgow."

"Got the paperwork?"

"Sure, but what—"

"We'll go pick your timber up for you in our truck." Fergal took the order receipt from her hand before she could protest. "Shouldn't be gone long."

"I can't ask you to do that."

"You're not asking, we're offering," Gus said.

Harley nodded. "You can repay us by feeding us tonight and letting us bunk down in one of your vacant rooms."

Briana hesitated. Did she really want them hanging around overnight? *Hell, yes!* Her head told her it was a seriously bad idea. Her body reacted very differently and sprang enthusiastically to life. Besides, if they got the timbers for her, her work schedule would be pretty much back on track. She might have naughty ideas about the three of them running through her head, but she very much doubted if they were similarly minded. They were just playing nice because they'd been paid to check up on her. Flirting seemed to come as naturally to them as breathing, and they couldn't seem to help honing their skills on her. Briana was levelheaded enough to know they couldn't really have designs of someone who looked like she did right now—splattered in plaster, her hair a mess, her clothing worse, her attitude ornery.

She was safe from them. She'd just have to rein in her wild fantasies about the three of them and make sure the same was true in reverse.

"Okay, thanks, you've got yourselves a deal."

Chapter Five

"She's hot!" Gus smacked his lips together as they drove away from the lodge. "I'm in *lurve*."

"Yeah, for once I agree with you, man," Harley said. "I'm betting she scrubs up real well."

"We need to keep this professional," Fergal said from behind the wheel.

"Yeah, like you're not fantasizing about jumping her bones," Gus replied. "I know you, buddy, and I saw the way you kept touching her every chance you got."

"You think she's a player, Ferg?" Harley asked.

"I'm not sure. She oozes sensuality, but I don't think she actually knows it."

"All the better," Gus replied. "I like awaking a woman's sensual side. Tell me you don't, Ferg."

Fergal hit the wheel with the heel of his hand and flashed a pained smile. "I'm trying real hard to remain objective here, but I gotta tell you, I'm getting vibes, too."

"Yes!" Gus and Harley shared a fist pump.

"Not so fast," Fergal said, laughing. "I don't want to put her under any obligation."

"Come on, Ferg." Harley shook his head. "We're just talking a bit of fun, if she's willing. I know you don't want commitment," he added, making inverted commas with his fingers around the word *commitment,* "and no one's suggesting that."

"We're here to do a job," Fergal reminded them. "Someone doesn't want her to succeed with what she's doing, and we need to figure out who, so we can straighten them out. In order to do that we need to find reasons to hang around until we get to the bottom of things, but that doesn't mean putting her under pressure to play with us."

Harley pulled a hard done by face. "You mean I can't tie her up and whip that cute butt until she begs me to fuck her?"

"She's already got your measure, buddy," Gus said. "She saw right through you when you came on to her."

"Nah, she already loves me."

Fergal shook his head. "You keep right on thinking that way, but bear in mind that she's damaged emotionally. Her mom running out on her like that and having a part-time father who probably seemed to love his career more than he loved her is enough to make anyone insecure. That's why she's adamant she doesn't want her dad interfering. She doesn't trust anyone because no one in her life, other than her grandmother, has given her any reason *to* trust."

"You saying we need to get her to trust us?" Harley asked.

"It would be a good place to start. Far as I can see, she's clinging to that lodge because it represents the only security she's ever known."

"You don't think she should do it?" Gus sounded surprised. "Seems to me she loves not just the lodge but the entire area."

"Sure I think she should keep the lodge, but she has a few demons to face up to first." Fergal paused. "And I know all about that shit," he added, almost to himself.

"She won't take kindly to us sticking around," Gus said. "She's too damned independent for her own good."

"She doesn't know what she's taken on, any more than she realizes someone's trying to fuck it up for her," Fergal replied.

"My money's on the jerk who ran us off the road," Harley said. "I reckon he's deliberately screwing things up for Briana so he can ride to her rescue. She'll fall at his feet with gratitude, and he'll get what he's always wanted, which is to marry her."

"Don't jump to conclusions, bud," Fergal said. "We'll check him out, and if he is behind it all, we'll pay him a friendly visit. I don't take kindly to being run off the road."

They found their way to the builders' merchants and, after a frustrating delay, the correct timber was found. The guys loaded it into the bed of their truck, secured it firmly in place, and headed back toward the lodge. As they drove through Fort Peck, Harley pointed out the barber shop.

"No gossipers outside at this hour," he remarked.

Gus, who gave the impression of being asleep in the backseat, pointed through the side window. "Well, well, look what we have here," he said.

Fergal and Harley following the direction of his finger and saw the SUV that had run them off the road earlier. A guy with sandy hair was leaning against the open driver's door, deep in conversation with another man. Harley snapped off a couple of quick shots of them on his cell phone. The two men finished their conversation, and the driver was about to climb into his car when he noticed them with the timber in the back of their truck. He shaded his eyes with his hand and took a long, hard look at them.

"Get down, Gus!" Fergal barked. "I don't want him to see you."

"Why not?" Gus asked, ducking down as ordered.

"I'm guessing that Romeo there knows who the timber's for. Briana said she'd told him earlier that it hadn't turned up. He must know someone around these parts with a truck, and if he really wants to help her, he could have offered to have it picked up. He didn't do that, which kinda makes you wonder."

"It sure does," Harley agreed. "You think he'll go to the lodge and check it out?"

"Nope, but I'm betting he'll be on his cell to Briana before the next signal changes."

They turned a corner at the end of the street, out of sight of Greg.

"You can get up now," Fergal said to Gus.

"So, you think this guy will call Briana and quiz her about us," Gus said. "Hope she has the sense to tell him to go fuck himself."

* * * *

Briana spent an hour finishing up her plastering, and then hit the shower. She absolutely wasn't doing so to make an impression upon her guests. Obviously she washed the muck off at the end every day, once she finished the grimy workload she'd set herself. Today she washed her hair as well, but only because she needed to get the dried plaster out of it. She really ought to get into the habit of wearing a hat when she worked.

"Okay, now what?"

Briana rummaged through her meager selection of clothing. Since she'd anticipated living on a glorified building site for the foreseeable future she'd only unpacked jeans and one pair of smart pants. Smart was out of the question. She didn't want to send out the wrong message, so clean jeans it would have to be. She paired them up with a long-sleeved T-shirt in a pale shade of green, thrust her feet into comfortable mules, and ran a brush through her damp hair. She'd leave it to its own devices, which meant it would dry into corkscrew curls that hung halfway down her back because that was who she was—wild and screwed up. Makeup was out of the question. So, too, was perfume.

"This is me," she told Max and the kittens. "Take me or leave me."

Briana made her way into the kitchen, wondering what to give the guys to eat. She had steaks in the freezer. Big men like them were bound to like steaks, so she took three out and set them in the microwave to defrost.

She's just thrown a salad together when the phone rang. It might be the guys calling with a problem about the timber, so she took the call.

"Hey, babe."

Shit, it was Greg! "Greg, how you doing?"

"Have you got visitors, or something?"

"Excuse me?"

"I saw some guys driving up to your place when I was leaving. I just wondered if you were okay."

"I'm a big girl, Greg," she said, trying her best to keep her temper in check. "I can take care of myself."

"I know that, honey. It's just that I care about you, stuck out there all on your own. Wouldn't want anyone taking advantage of you."

Briana exhaled. She knew that was true, although she suspected it was more than that. She'd stupidly been out with him a couple of times since his divorce, believing him when he said he wanted to be just friends. Was it ever possible for a man and a woman to be *just friends,* especially when they had a history? She suspected now that he wanted more than that and had no intention of encouraging him, persistent though he was. She also had no reason not to tell him about the guys.

"They're friends of my dad's, just stopped by to say hello."

"I see."

Greg didn't sound happy about that. She wouldn't put it past him to come on out and check up on her, so Briana explained. "They've done me a favor and run over to the builders' merchants to pick up that timber for me."

"That's kind of them. I should have thought to arrange it myself. I guess they'll be gone once they drop it off."

"Yeah, they will." That ought to satisfy him. "Anyway, if there's nothing else you need to know, I have stuff to do."

"Sure I can't tempt you out to dinner this evening?"

"Absolutely. Gotta go."

Briana cut the connection. The guys would be back any time now. Hell, she hadn't made up beds for them. She ran back to the bedroom wing, found sheets and blankets, and made up one room with a double bed and another with two singles. No prizes for guessing who'd take the double, she thought, rolling her eyes. She put fresh towels in the only working bathroom. All four of them would have to share. Well, at least the door had a decent lock.

Briana stifled a yawn, only just realizing how tired she was. She'd been up since dawn and hadn't stopped all day. She now had three guests to entertain and wouldn't last another hour unless she closed her eyes—just for a moment or two.

She went back to her room, lay on top of her bed, and was asleep within seconds.

* * * *

Fergal stopped the truck outside the wing of the lodge without a roof. Might as well unload the timber where it was needed. The three of them completed the task with swift economy, stashing it in the shed close to the roof slates. Fergal was surprised Briana didn't hear them and come out to make sure everything was all right. When they entered the lodge and there was still no sign of her, he became concerned.

"There are steaks defrosted in the microwave," Gus said, heading straight for the kitchen, "and she's made a salad. She must be here somewhere."

Fergal found her, lying on her bed, dead to the world. His cock stirred at the sight of her hair spread across the pillow beneath her like a fiery halo. She was one hell of a beautiful woman, and he'd always had a thing for redheads. The temptation to lean down and kiss her awake was compelling, but Fergal couldn't take the chance of spooking her.

He crept from the room and closed the door as quietly as he could, leaving her to sleep.

"She's sound asleep," he said to the others.

Gus, busy preparing their supper, stuck his head around the kitchen door. "Aw, she must be beat."

"Go get some logs in," Fergal told Harley. "The evenings still get cold around here."

Harley trotted off to do as he was told. Fergal found some kindling and started to build a fire in the huge grate. By the time Harley returned with a basketful of logs, Fergal already had a blaze going.

"I think I saw some candles in the dining room," Fergal said. "Let's get the dust sheets off this furniture, get some candles going, and create a real homely atmosphere for when she wakes up."

"You *are* thinking what I'm thinking," Harley accused. "About time you came down off that moral high ground and admitted you want her as much as we do."

"I want her to relax," Fergal replied. "There's stuff she's not telling us, I'm sure of it."

The three of them worked like the compact unit they'd always been—Gus in the kitchen, Fergal and Harley transforming the lounge into something closer to the room that Briana recalled from her younger days. There was nothing they could do about the bare-plaster walls, but low lighting and a roaring fire worked in their favor.

"I like it," Harley said, plumping up the cushions on a big old armchair and then throwing himself into it.

"Yeah." Fergal nodded.

"What the devil—"

The men glanced at the doorway and saw Briana standing there, corkscrew curls tumbling over her shoulders, her eyes still heavy with sleep.

"We didn't want to disturb you," Fergal said. "You looked kinda beat."

"I can't believe I slept for so long." She glanced around the room. "This looks so inviting. Thanks, but dinner, I ought to—"

"Gus has got it covered." Fergal patted the seat beside him. "Take a load off. We came prepared with beer and wine. Which would you prefer?"

"Wine." She shot him a grateful smile. "I haven't seen any of that for a while."

"You've just got time for one glass," Gus said, sticking his head out of the kitchen door. "Then we'll eat."

"Good," she said. "I'm famished, but it doesn't seem right letting you guys wait on me."

"It's what we do best," Harley said. "We're well trained."

She laughed. "So I see."

Fergal handed her a brimming glass of white wine. She thanked him, took a healthy sip, and nodded appreciatively. "I could get used to this."

"All part of the service, ma'am."

"I haven't even asked you if you got the timber."

"No problems. Your guys can get started tomorrow."

"I'm real grateful to you."

"Food's up," Gus said, carrying serving dishes through to the dining room.

Fergal helped Briana to her feet, and they all followed Gus. The table was set for the four of them, more candles burning on every surface, wine in a cooler. Briana, seated between Fergal and Gus, cut into her steak, took a bite, and closed her eyes in appreciation.

"Where did you learn to cook?" she asked Gus. "This is delicious."

"My dad's a chef, and the family has a couple of restaurants, so I guess I was raised to appreciate good food. Then, in the marines, it was either take over the catering whenever I got the chance or accept third best." Briana twirled one of her crazy curls around her finger, her gaze fixed on Gus's face as he chatted about his culinary skills and sent her the occasional sinful smile. Fergal watched her, thinking she probably didn't realize that she was responding to his buddy's lazy, persuasive charm in the exact same way that most women did when he bothered to turn it on. "I like to eat well so, hanging out with these two, I have no choice but to be chief cook and bottle washer."

"What *do* the three of you do?" she asked. "Presumably you're not in the service anymore."

"We live in Columbus Falls," Fergal told her.

"Oh, I didn't realize you were from this state."

"Originally we're from all over," Harley told her, "but we served together, share lots of…er, interests in common, and so it seemed sensible to stay together."

"Oh." She covered her mouth with her hand and blushed deeply. "I didn't realize—"

"Not those sorts of interests," Fergal said. "We're not gay, if that's what you're thinking, we're simply business partners."

"We're ski instructors in the winter," Gus told her. "In the summer we lead orienteering treks in the mountains, stuff like that. It's what we're trained to do, and we're good at it, though I do say so myself."

"You're like me then," she replied. "You enjoy being outside, close to nature."

"Absolutely," they all said together.

"That was really good, Gus, thanks," Briana said, pushing her empty plate aside. "I can't remember the last time I ate so much."

"Glad it met with your approval, ma'am."

"I'll clear the dishes."

"No you won't." Gus took her elbow and helped her from her chair. "I cook, these guys clean up after me, that's the rule."

"Yes, but I can still help. I was supposed to cook for you, remember?"

"They can manage. They're big boys."

"Hmm," Briana said, making Fergal think that she'd probably noticed that for herself but didn't wish to say so.

"It also means I get to sit by the fire and have you all to myself for a while," Gus added.

Briana laughed. "Seems only fair."

Fergal was pleased when she responded to Gus's flirtatious tone in like manner. It implied that she was starting to relax around them. Better yet, there had been no further talk of them leaving since they'd gotten back from collecting the timber. Gus could build on the start they'd made with her while he and Harley cleared up the kitchen. They had a way to go with her yet, so it was probably better not to crowd her or come on too strong. She was fiercely independent *and* emotionally damaged. Fergal reminded himself that they weren't there to make things more complicated for her.

Her phone rang before she even made it back to the great room. She picked it up, listened to what was being said, and Fergal could tell from her stricken expression that it was bad news.

"What's happened?" he asked when she ended the call.

"My guys can't start on the roof tomorrow," she replied, thumping the back of a chair in obvious frustration. "Someone's ratted them out to the IRS."

Chapter Six

"What the fuck?" Fergal shared her anger. "I didn't see that one coming."

Briana shrugged, trying hard not to show just how badly this latest blow had affected her. "The way my luck's been running with this project, nothing surprises me anymore."

"What did your guys say?"

"Their boss got a call from the local IRS office. Supposedly it was just a friendly warning telling him he'd be held responsible if his employees were caught working anywhere for cash in hand." She looked at each of them in turn, shaking her head. "How could they know?"

"They're pissing in the wind, darlin'," Harley said, looking as angry as Fergal obviously felt. These guys weren't comfortable to be around when they got mad, Briana was fast discovering.

"Agreed." A muscle in Fergal's jaw flexed and hardened. "It's total bullshit. The guys hadn't even started working for you yet, so if they *had* been reported it could only have been recently. Contrary to popular belief, the IRS simply doesn't react that fast. Nor do they issue *friendly* warnings. Someone's yanking your chain, sweetheart."

"How do they know the call even came from the IRS?" Gus asked.

"Oh, I didn't think to ask." She frowned. "But who else would it be?"

"How long have you got?" Fergal replied.

Their reaction ought to have calmed her, but it had the opposite effect. She felt tears brimming and was determined not to cry in front of them. Briana *never* cried. Crying for her mama when she'd been a little girl, scared of the dark, had gotten her nowhere. Her daddy was never around to make things better, so she'd learned to bottle her emotions up, put on a tough front, and never allowed anyone to see how badly she was hurting.

Never allowed anyone to get too close.

She'd tried to explain her feelings to Greg when he'd accused her of being cold-hearted. He knew her better than anyone—had supposedly wanted to marry her—but seemed to think she could shake off her bitterness about her mother's betrayal and get on with life like it was no big deal. His reaction taught her an important lesson, and she'd never attempted to explain her commitment issues to anyone else since then. Bury the hurt, slap on a smile, and keep it all bottled up. That had always worked for Briana. It would work again now.

She'd get through this latest setback. Somehow. She bounced back every time something went wrong with her project, her enthusiasm and determination overcoming all roadblocks set in her path. She would draw on that strength and overcome this problem, too.

Except this felt like one disaster too many, and it was beyond her to cope. She was tired of coping, of trying to remain positive while always playing catch-up. Perhaps the wine was responsible for her sudden fit of self-pity, or maybe too little sleep over a long period was finally taking its toll. Either way, tears were perilously close. She needed to get out of here in case she couldn't control them. The guys would never let her be if she went all girly on them and broke down.

"Excuse me," she said, heading for her room at a run.

She slammed the door behind her, assuming none of them would follow her over the threshold. Stupid mistake! These guys clearly didn't understand the concept of privacy, and when the door opened again almost immediately, it occurred to her that she should have locked herself in the bathroom instead. She looked up and saw Fergal leaning against the door jamb, arms folded across his impressive torso, looking like he'd just stepped off the pages of a magazine.

"I just need a private minute," she said.

"It ain't so bad, darlin'."

He spoke in a softly hypnotic cadence, not budging from his spot in the open doorway where his broad shoulder appeared to be holding up the wall. The warm richness of his penetrating gaze sent her emotions into free fall. She was unable to dash the tears away before he saw them, but it no longer seemed to matter. He appeared unbothered that they were alone in her bedroom, which is when Briana realized that her emotions had undergone a sea change. Two minutes ago her problems seemed like the end of the world. Now she wasn't even thinking about them. How could she when fiery vibes flew between them as their gazes clashed and the silence intensified. She became increasingly aware of the powerful aura that clung to him, like he could achieve anything he set his mind to because it wouldn't occur to him that failure was an option.

She blamed the charged atmosphere, his hungry gaze, and her turbulent emotions when her thoughts flew to sex. It seemed to happen whenever she was alone with any of them and was so untypical of her that it helped bring her to her senses.

"Easy for you to say," she replied, grabbing a tissue from the box on the dresser and blowing her nose.

"You just need to be strong, and we'll get to the bottom of who's doing this to you."

Briana blinked back her surprise. "You think someone's deliberately—"

"I'm sure of it." He reached for her hand. "Come on, let's go in the other room and talk this through. Between us we ought to be able to figure it out."

"Oh."

She'd thought he was going to kiss her. Instead he just wanted to talk. So much for the mutual attraction she thought she'd sensed between them. Briana bit back her disappointment and slipped her hand into his outstretched one. She felt the same rush of heat fuel her body as had happened the first time their hands had touched. His fingers closed around her hand, and he smiled down at her, his eyes alight with an elusive warmth that encouraged trust.

"Hey, babe, that was a neat trick you pulled there," Gus said, sticking his head around the kitchen door. "Fergal will grab any excuse to get out of the clearing up."

Briana actually laughed. "Sorry," she said, falling into the corner of the settee and accepting another glass of wine from Fergal. Harley came in from outside with another basket of logs and threw a couple onto the dwindling fire.

"Tell me why you think this is more than just bad luck," she said, once all three guys were seated around her. She glanced at Harley and quickly glanced away again. His impressive physique at such close quarters made it hard to keep her mind on the subject. That was kind of crazy given it was her livelihood under threat and that nothing mattered to her more than knocking the lodge back into shape.

"Has to be," Fergal replied. "Did your friend Greg call you while we were out this afternoon?"

"Yes, but if you think—"

"What did he want?" Gus asked.

"Actually, he asked about you guys. Wanted to know who you were and why you were here."

"None of his fucking business," Harley snarled.

"He was only looking out for me."

"Sure he was," Fergal said drolly. "Did you tell him we'd gone to collect the timber?"

"Yes, but that doesn't mean anything."

"You're awfully keen to defend him," Fergal replied, his eyes now flat and hard. "You sure there's nothing you need to tell us about your relationship with him?"

"Quite sure." She folded her arms in a defensive gesture that probably made her look guilty. "Why would Greg want to see me fail?"

"So he can ride to the rescue, put everything right, and earn your eternal gratitude," Harley said with a cynical twist of his lips.

"That's stupid."

"His call also came in immediately after he saw us driving through Fort Peck with a truck load of timber," Gus said, shaking his head. "Coincidence? I don't think so."

"Do you recognize this guy with him?" Harley asked, showing her the pictures he'd taken with his cell phone.

Briana studied them carefully and shook her head. "No, I don't think so. He's half-turned away from the camera, so I can't be sure. Should I know him?"

"It's probably nothing," Harley replied, taking his phone back.

"Greg wants you back," Fergal said, picking up a strand of her hair and winding it casually around his finger. She was about to snatch it back when his knuckled brushed against her neck. She gasped, unable to believe the raw need that coursed through her at such an innocent connection. "Seems to me he'll go to just about any lengths to get you, as well. Not that I blame him, but I don't like the way he's going about it. He ought to be a man and do things right."

"You're wrong about him. He's harmless."

"He also has a powerful father and an influential job," Fergal pointed out.

"Who would profit if you failed?" Gus asked.

"No one. I guess the people who want to buy the lodge will—"

"Someone wants to buy it?" three voices asked together.

"And you didn't think that was relevant?" Fergal added alone.

"Hey, cut me some slack!" She pushed her hands in front of her, palms outward, as though warding off an attack. "It was a while back and I'd forgotten all about it. Gran got a couple of offers from a guy based in Denver. She turned them down and he went away. Then, after Gran died, he approached me with a pretty reasonable offer, but—"

"But you turned him down, too," Fergal finished for her. "Who was he and what did he want the place for?"

"Some businessman who wanted a place to get away from it all."

"It's not exactly a little lakeside cabin he could use for a weekend retreat," Gus pointed out, his gaze encompassing the huge room.

"Well, what can I say? People with money have different standards, I guess."

"What was his reaction when you turned him down?" Harley asked.

"He was fine about it. I didn't speak with him direct, of course. I dealt with his real estate broker, who said his client had other properties in mind, thanked me for my time, and that was that. It was all so amiable that I'd forgotten about it."

"Do you have his name?" Gus asked. "Any details?"

"Yes, I'll find them for you. They're still around somewhere, because the broker said if I ever changed my mind, to get back in touch. Not that I will, but you know."

"We do." She noticed Fergal share a speaking glance with his buddies. "Anyway, you don't need to worry about your lost workforce. We'll do the roof for you."

She sat bolt upright, pulling her hair out of Fergal's hand. "You! I can't ask you to do that. Besides…well, do you even know how? It's skilled work."

"We're highly trained professionals," Gus said, winking at her. "We can do anything we set our minds to."

"And you don't have to pay us, so the IRS won't get involved," Fergal added.

She shook her head. "I don't know what to say."

Fergal leaned down and kissed the top of her head. "Our pleasure."

"You guys are a little intimidating, if you don't mind my saying so. Seems there's nothing you can't do."

"Honey, you have no idea," Harley said, leaning in from her other side and also kissing the top of her head.

"Hey, that ain't fair," Gus protested from his position on the floor. "When do I get to have a kiss?"

Briana laughed, feeling light-headed and emotionally overloaded. This wasn't happening. She'd wake up soon and be back to reality. No way could these three hunks be fighting over her.

"What can I do for you guys in return?" she asked. "There must be something you want."

* * * *

Fergal shared another look with his buddies, and they both nodded imperceptibly. They would know what he was thinking, mainly because they'd be thinking it, too, and had just given him the green light. Even so, he could see they were surprised that he'd allowed this assignment to get so personal this fast. Hell, *he* was surprised. He had no idea what madness drew him toward Briana, but something stronger than his own will was making him act out of character. This time the line between business and pleasure would be crossed, if she'd allow it.

Her back was turned slightly toward him, and he took the opportunity to push her hair aside and place his hands on her shoulders.

"What are you doing?" she asked, sounding anxious.

"Getting rid of some of the kinks. You're wound up tighter than an enemy sniper, darlin'. Just relax into my hands and let me sort you out."

Fergal wasn't surprised when she resisted him at first. She had problems with ceding control to anyone. He almost laughed at that. If she agreed to play with the three of them, then one thing she would *never* have was control. His cock stirred as he thought about the sorts of things he'd have her do. Those sweet lips of hers sure would look pretty wrapped around his cock while one of his buddies paddled her ass and the other teased her fat nipples between his teeth. Or perhaps he'd do that. Fergal was a tit man through and through, and hers were a damned sight more tempting than they had any right to be.

Down boy! Fergal was getting ahead of himself and so he took his frustration out on her tightly knotted muscles until she rolled her shoulders and groaned with pleasure. She closed her eyes and rotated her neck, almost purring with relief.

"Something else you're good at," she murmured.

Fergal shifted so that he was leaning in the corner of the couch, and she was obliged to bring her feet up onto it. Harley lifted her legs and placed them on his lap. Her eyes flew open, but when Harley started to gently massage her instep, she emitted a little sigh and closed them again.

"You enjoying this?" Fergal asked, watching Harley work on her toes, one at a time.

"Hmm." She didn't open her eyes. "Keep this up and I'll be asleep."

Gus slid closer to her from his position on the floor and covered her lips fleetingly with his own. He broke the kiss almost before it had begun and glanced up triumphantly at Fergal and Harley. All three of them knew then that Briana would play with them—not through some misplaced sense of gratitude, but because they were awakening the sensual side of her nature and she was curious.

"Come on, darlin'," Fergal said, his words causing Harley to quit massaging her toes and for Gus to stop running his fingers gently across her rib cage. "You look beat. Time you were tucked up in bed."

"Hmm," she said again, still not opening her eyes. "Don't want to be alone."

"Tomorrow night we'll have a little party, the four of us," Fergal promised her. "You think you might like that?"

Finally her eyes opened. "What sort of party?"

"We three live, work, and play together," he replied softly. "We like to share."

"And we want to share you, if you'll let us," Harley said.

"Doesn't matter if you don't want to," Gus said, rising athletically from the floor. "We'll still do your roof and make sure you get the lodge back on track."

"No reason why we can't have some fun along the way," Fergal added.

Briana sat up and blinked. "You three all want to fuck me. Is that what you're saying?"

"Pretty much," Fergal confirmed, dropping his head to capture a brief kiss. "But before you decide, you need to understand that we like to be in charge."

Her eye-roll was accompanied by a sinful smile, as though she'd just realized how much power she actually wielded over them. "Why am I not surprised?"

"What Fergal is making a poor job of saying," Gus told her, "is that we'd like to tie you up, spank that cute ass, and…er, stuff like that."

"I'm not big on pain."

"Ah, but when you know how to channel that pain, it'll blow your mind," Harley said. "And we'll teach you all you need to know."

She glanced at each of them in turn, her eyes shimmering with awareness. "You need to understand that I'm not very experienced."

"Music to our ears," Gus replied.

"I've only ever been with two men. Greg, and then there was a guy in Florida for a while, but it didn't work out."

"Better yet," Fergal said, standing up and sweeping her into his arms. "If you're saying *yes*, then we'll teach you everything you need to know."

"I'm saying *yes*."

Gus and Harley shared a high five. Fergal brushed the hair away from her brow, kissed it chastely, and carried her toward her bedroom.

"We'll let this guy out," Gus said, indicating Max.

Just as well because Briana, terrible mother that she was, had forgotten all about him.

"You need to get your beauty sleep, darlin'," Fergal said as he deposited her on her bed, still fully clothed, and winked at her. "Sleep late in the morning and save your energy. Trust me, you're gonna need it."

Chapter Seven

Three large male bodies crowded around her when Gus and Harley returned with Max.

"We'd sure like to stay, undress you, and tuck you in," Gus said. "But if we did that, you'd never get any sleep."

Sleep? Who needed to sleep? What the hell did they think they were playing at anyway? Getting her all steamed up and then leaving her with vague promises about tomorrow being another day. There was a name for women who did that sort of stuff. Did it work in reverse? Pussy teasers, that's what they were. They'd set hers on fire and now planned to leave her alone. *So* not fair.

"Just a minute."

Three heads turned to look at her. "Yes," Fergal said.

"You can't...I mean, you can't just make promises and then not deliver."

"Oh, we'll deliver, honey, on that you have my solemn word." Fergal sent her a sexy smile that made her feel weak at the knees, and other places. "But first we have a roof to fix and your problems to sort."

"The two don't need to be mutually exclusive." God, she sounded like she was begging now.

"We need you to think about our suggestion and come to a decision without any pressure from us," Fergal said.

But I want you to pressure me!

"Just remember to sleep as late as you like," Harley said as they left the room and he closed the door behind them.

Shit, they really did mean to leave her be. And as for sleeping late, who were they kidding? Briana ducked into the bathroom to brush her teeth and splash water over her heated face. Then she returned to her room, threw off her clothes, and slid naked between crisp cotton sheets that had been lovingly laundered a thousand times in her grandmother's day. She had a ton of stuff to do at first light and couldn't afford the luxury of sleeping late. She didn't bother to argue with Fergal, mainly because she knew that in a clash of wills with such a strong alpha she'd always come out on the losing side. She'd pretend to agree with them and then go her own way. The three of them might think they were in charge in the bedroom, but her life outside of it was still her own to dictate.

The bedroom.

Her pussy leaked when she thought of what she'd just so brazenly agreed to do. What she'd wanted to do ever since setting eyes on the three of them, shameless hussy that she was. They were no-strings-attached kind of guys, and that suited Briana just fine. She didn't do emotion, either. She hadn't told them that sex didn't do much for her, or that she'd never achieved orgasm through penetration. In fact, her best orgasms had been self-induced. Even though she'd only had two lovers, she'd discovered that the male ego was a delicate creature. To avoid wounded masculine pride or elongated efforts to prove themselves, she'd become a pretty good actress.

She wondered why she felt such a gravitational pull toward all three of them when she knew she wouldn't derive the ultimate satisfaction from whatever they did to her. Still, what you've never had you can't miss. Just about every woman she knew entered into casual sexual liaisons almost as frequently as they shopped for shoes, but Briana had never been tempted to follow their example. Until now. She smiled to herself. Looked like she was about to make up plenty of lost ground.

She turned over and curled into a tight ball, squeezing her thighs together as liquid squirted from her pussy and anticipation coursed through her veins, making her body come alive in spite of the fact that she was bone weary. They'd turned her on without touching any of her more sensitive places, and she was having a hard job finding the off switch. Briana was sorely tempted to fish her vibrator out of the bedside drawer and press it into service, but resisted. She might not be able to orgasm through penetrative sex but had no trouble coming when her clit was agitated or, better yet, sucked into submission. Presumably one of them would be willing to perform that service, and she guessed they wouldn't need a map to find their way around her body.

The wine and the excitement of the day took their toll, and Briana fell asleep with images of her three fine-looking house guests filling her head. Her last conscious thought was about her ability to accommodate them. She'd seen the impressive bulges in the front of their pants, but her pussy was narrow and tight. *What the hell, it's designed to stretch, right?*

Reassured, she slept remarkably well but still awoke at first light.

Except it wasn't.

Briana sat bolt upright when the sunlight streaming through the open drapes warmed her face. Judging by the sun's position in the sky, it had to be at least ten in the morning. One glance at her bedside clock confirmed her estimate. Hell, why hadn't Max woken her? He must be desperate for a pee. She called her dog, but he didn't respond because he no longer appeared to be in the room. One of the guys had to have let him out and she hadn't even noticed.

Briana threw back the covers, had a sixty-second shower, and jumped into her clothes. The great room was deserted, but the smell of freshly brewed coffee led her to the kitchen. She poured herself a cup and noticed a plate of warm muffins sitting on the counter. One of them must have driven over to the bakery. How did they know blueberry muffins were her absolute favorite?

She munched on one and went outside to look for them. What she found caused her to stop dead in her tracks. All three of them were up on the roof, stripped to the waist as they removed the rotten timbers, tossing them to the ground like they weighed nothing at all. Worn denim jeans clung to slim hips and long, toned legs. Rock-hard torsos glistened with sweat, muscles rippled and flexed as they worked seamlessly as a team. They wore no safety equipment but walked about on those rotting beams with lithe grace, slick coordination, and seemingly no concerns for their welfare. She wanted to warn them to be careful, but the words stuck in her throat. They were too proficient to fall. She shivered, wondering if that was true in the bedroom also.

Before they saw her, Briana absolutely had to get her camera. They were the ones who'd suggested selling her work. If the sight of these three half-naked Adonises didn't produce results spectacular enough to get the ladies flexing the plastic then Briana would take up knitting.

She grabbed her Pentax, spent a few moments fiddling with lenses, made all the necessary adjustments, and started snapping away. She caught them unawares from a dozen different angles before Fergal noticed her. She guiltily lowered her camera, having just caught him from behind when he was leaning over to heave up a beam. Wow!

"Morning," he said cheerfully. "Sleep well?"

"You should have woken me."

"Why?" Harley asked. "You wanna come up here and help?"

"I could have made breakfast, at least."

"You don't need to look after us, babe," Gus said, wiping sweat from his brow and blowing her a kiss. "We can take care of ourselves."

"Obviously. And thanks for the muffins." Max came trotting up to her, a piece of discarded timber in his mouth, tail wagging. "Hey, buddy," she said, rubbing his ears. "You being good?"

"We fed him, and the kittens," Fergal said.

"Er, thanks." Her discomfort had to be pretty damned obvious because he had the audacity to grin. "How's it going up there?"

"No problems. We've almost got all the old timbers out. Then we'll start fixing the new ones in place. Should get half of them done today."

So soon? "That's good," she said distractedly. Briana could stand where she was all day, simply admiring the view. "I'd best be getting back to my plastering then."

"Good plan."

Plastering usually gave Briana considerable satisfaction. Today it just seemed laborious. Her thoughts were taken up by the guys walking about on her roof with all the lithe grace of large felines. No mention had been made of their proposition, but then that was hardly the sort of thing that could be shouted about, she supposed, even if there was no one around to overhear them. Hopefully they hadn't had a change of heart and wouldn't been too tired after a day's full work to…well, to work on her. Briana giggled, wondering what had become of the levelheaded, single-minded Briana who never wasted time on impossible daydreams.

The phone jolted her out of her erotic fantasy—the one where Gus was kissing her, Harley was sucking her toes, and Fergal—hell, don't go there! She snatched up the phone, aware that her panties were already soaked clean through.

"Hello."

"Hey, Briana, I just heard about the roofers. That sucks."

Shit! It was Greg commiserating about her latest setback. After the insinuations the guys had made last night, she was immediately suspicious of his motives.

"Bad news travels fast."

"It'll blow over, honey. Give the dust some time to settle and then I'm sure the guys will be happy to help you out."

They both knew she couldn't afford to wait. "Sure."

"You don't seem too bothered by it."

"Shit happens, Greg. I'm learning to take the rough with the smooth. Isn't that what you've always advised?"

"Oh...er, yes, I guess." He sounded suspicious, which is when Briana knew she'd played it all wrong. He'd be out here in no time to check things out, and she really didn't want him to know that the guys were still here. He'd get all proprietary, simply because she'd never bothered to stop him acting that way before. It hadn't seemed to matter. In the future she'd be firmer in her determination to remain independent. After the guys had gone. Especially then.

"Your visitors get away okay?" he asked.

"I've gotta run, Greg. My plaster will dry out if I leave it too long."

She hung up, wondering what she'd just set in motion.

* * * *

Fergal heaved the last of the rotted timbers off the edge of the roof and stood up to wipe the sweat away from his brow.

"Okay, that about does it," he said, stating the obvious. "Let's break for lunch. We can start fixing in the new timbers after that. You did check that they've been cut to the right length, Harley?"

"Yeah, I told you I had when you asked me the last time."

They each slid nimbly down the ladder. Fergal slapped Harley's shoulder when they were all back on the ground.

"Sorry, buddy." He turned toward Gus. "You made that call to Raoul, right?"

"Yeah, yeah. He's gonna check up on this Greg character, and the nature of his father's business."

"Good. Let's hope we hear back from him soon." Fergal scowled. "I'm convinced this is all a grand scheme to win Briana's undying gratitude, but we need to make sure it's nothing more sinister."

Harley laughed. "And what we're doing isn't?"

"You think we need to renovate the lady's house to get inside her pants?"

"Tetchy! Can't imagine what he's so worked up for, can you?" Gus asked Harley, grinning.

"Just so we're clear," Fergal said, halting his buddies before they went into the house, "if she's had a change of heart, we are *not* going to put any pressure on her. Understood?"

Harley shot him a look. "What do you take us for? When did we ever talk a woman into doing something she didn't want to do?"

"Yeah, I know, I'm sorry. I guess she's special and I—"

"She must be," Gus said, serious for once. "Otherwise you wouldn't have left things the way we did last night."

"Yeah, when did we last walk *out* of a willing woman's bedroom?" Harley asked.

"She's carrying a lot of emotional baggage. I just don't want to screw her head up any more than it already is."

Harley and Gus shared a look. "Right. That would be it," Harley said.

"Admit it, buddy," Gus said. "She's different and she's gotten under your skin."

"Don't read more into this than exists," Fergal replied as they walked into the house. "She's hot and I want her. End of."

"Hey, babe, you needn't have done that," Gus said, looking at the platter of sandwiches awaiting them and breathing in the aroma of what was obviously chicken soup simmering on the stove.

"It was the least I could do," she replied. "There's iced tea or coffee if you'd prefer."

"Coffee's good," Fergal said. "We'll just wash up."

Fergal watched Briana without making it obvious as they gathered around the kitchen counter and ate their lunch. She seemed nervous and wouldn't look at any one of them directly in the eye.

"Heard from Greg?" he asked.

"Yes, he called this morning as it happens to commiserate about the roofers not turning up."

"I'll just bet he did," Fergal said, flexing his jaw. "Did you tell him we'd stepped into their shoes?"

"No, I figured he didn't need to know that." Finally she looked straight at him, and what Fergal saw reflected in her remarkable eyes hit him squarely below the belt. His cock swelled in a way that only arousal or desire in a woman's expression usually evoked. But Briana's eyes didn't intimate anything sexual. Instead they displayed total trust in his abilities, making him feel like he could conquer the world. Shit, he was in trouble! His buddies thought he felt, actually felt, something for Briana. He'd tried to deny it, to himself as much as to them, but knew in his heart it was true. The hard shell he'd erected around his emotions had thawed, and she'd had the temerity to slither right on in between the cracks to mess with his immaculately organized existence. She didn't know it yet, but such brazen behavior would earn her a good spanking later on. "Did I do right?"

"What? Oh yeah, babe, exactly right. What's the betting that he turns up here later to lend you a shoulder?"

"Most likely," she conceded with a wry smile.

He arrived when the guys had only been back at work for half an hour. Fergal heard the steady thrumping of his SUV's engine long before they actually saw it.

"Down!" he said to his buddies. "It's showtime."

The three of them slid down the ladder and concealed themselves from view. This was Briana's party, and they'd only intercede if they were needed. Greg slowed when he drove onto the property and saw the roof had been stripped. Without getting out of his car to investigate, he drove straight up to the front door, killed his engine, and finally exited the vehicle.

"Hey, Briana."

"Greg?"

She came out of the house, wearing her plaster-splattered clothing. Fergal wasn't close enough to see her expression but could tell from her abrupt response that she wasn't pleased to see him.

"What brings you out here again?" she asked.

"I was worried. What happened to the roof? I thought the guys couldn't help."

"I found someone else."

"Who?"

"Thanks for your concern, but it's really none of your business."

"Don't be like that, honey."

"Like what?"

"You've gone all secretive on me. I don't like that."

"You'll get over it."

"Attagirl!" Fergal muttered.

"You weren't quite so coy when we had dinner together the other night."

"What?" Fergal shared a glance with his buddies and shook his head. "I thought she didn't have anything to do with the creep."

"She obviously told us what we wanted to hear," Gus replied.

"Don't jump to conclusions, guys," Harley said. "Dinner doesn't mean anything."

"How would the IRS have heard that I was hiring Ben and Joe to do the roof?" she asked. "Any ideas?"

"How do they hear anything?" Greg kicked at a loose stone. "They have eyes and ears everywhere."

"He's lying," Fergal muttered. "He can't meet her gaze."

"Yes, but only Ben and Joe, you, and me knew about it."

"Well then, one of them must have said something." Greg sounded worried. "Or, more like, Seth and Maurice got to hear about it and said something at the barber shop. You know how nothing gets past them."

"Yes, that must be it."

"So, are you going to invite me in for some iced tea? It sure is a hot day."

"Sorry, Greg, if you want tea you should have stayed in town. I don't have time for socializing."

"What's happened to you, darlin'? You used to be glad to see me."

"I am glad to see you, Greg. I just don't have time to linger."

"Come on." He stepped forward and tried to take Briana's arm. "You and I are an item. Always have been and always will be. Okay, so we were too young for each other right out of college, but that's not the case anymore. Let me help you. You know I want to. I worry about you, stuck out here all alone."

"Let me go, Greg. You're hurting my arm."

"Just tell me what's going on."

"Stay out of sight," Fergal said to Gus as he and Harley stepped out to help her.

"Leave me be!" She shook her arm free and glowered at him.

"What's wrong with you today?" He grabbed her arm again. "You never used to be such a cock tease."

"Ouch!"

"The lady asked you to let her go," Fergal said in a glacial tone.

"Who the fuck are you?"

"It's okay," Briana said, shaking his hand off again. "Greg was just leaving."

"These are the jerks with the truck." Greg nodded toward the vehicle in question, only now appearing to notice it parked alongside Briana's car. "You told me they'd left."

"No, you made that assumption. I just didn't bother to put you straight."

"You don't need strangers hanging about, babe. You have no idea who they are or what they want from you."

"Not your concern."

"The hell it isn't!"

"Just go," she said wearily.

"Okay, but I'll call you later."

"Leave it, Greg. You weren't there for me when I needed you. Now I've got all the help I can handle."

Fergal wanted to applaud. Instead he and Harley adopted the stance—legs slightly apart, arms held loosely at their sides—ready to counter any move Greg might make in an effort to impress Briana. Fortunately for him, he wasn't quite that stupid. He glanced over his shoulder at them as he made his way back to his car, frowning like he bore the entire world a grudge.

"Well," Fergal said, watching him turn his car and drive away. "If he's behind the sabotage, I think we just called his bluff."

Chapter Eight

Briana indulged in a long soak in the bath, excitement ripping through her as she thought about the evening ahead of her. The kittens had sneaked in with her and were playing a game, diving in and out of the wicker laundry basket, destroying it with their sharp claws. Briana barely noticed. Instead she critically examined her naked body, noting its many flaws. Her gut wasn't quite flat, her tits were too large, she absolutely hated her knees, and they probably didn't realize that the freckles across her nose were replicated across her entire body. Hot properties such as them would be used to perfection, and they'd probably have a change of heart when they saw her in the raw.

"Am I really going to do this?" she asked the kittens. They continued causing mayhem with her grandmother's old laundry basket and had no answer to give. "Fat lot of help you two are."

They seemed deadly serious—the guys, not the kittens. Even though no mention was made until they finished work for the day, she could tell from the hungry expressions in Gus's and Harley's eyes that they were still very much up for it. Fergal was harder to read. Since Greg's impromptu visit he'd been quiet and withdrawn. It seemed they were all dancing around the subject, and she grew tired of waiting for them to raise it.

"What do I have to do?" she asked when they quit work for the day, addressing the question to Fergal.

"You absolutely sure? No pressure."

"I'm sure."

Was she? She was again reminded that she'd never had casual sex with anyone. She thought she'd been in love with both the men she'd

given herself to, which made it okay. She felt very different about
these three. It obviously wasn't possible to be in love with three
people at once. Was it? All she knew was that they'd brought her
staid old self to life without laying an inappropriate finger on her.
They'd only be here for twenty-four hours, but it seemed like a hell of
a lot longer than that and she had no intention of wasting precious
time by pretending to be coy. *Bring it on, guys!* They didn't need to
know that her emotions were involved, which they would be. It was
different for women, she reasoned. They couldn't approach intimacy
with the same detached attitude as men did.

"Go and have a nice long soak in the bath," Harley had told her.
"Gus has already run it for you. It ought to be about ready."

"I can't waste time soaking in the bath." Where did they get off on
telling her what to do? She wasn't a marine under their command.

"Sure you can, honey. I'll see to dinner, Fergal will get the fire
going, and by the time you're ready to eat, you won't know the
place." He patted her butt. "Now scoot."

She didn't know the bathroom, either. Gus had left the main light
off and lit candles everywhere. The fragrance of bath oil assailed her
nostrils, and she already felt herself relaxing. She threw off her dirty
clothes and sank into the water, groaning with pleasure as she felt the
tension draining out of her.

She could do this. She absolutely could.

Briana drifted off to sleep, until the water cooled and jolted her
awake again. She climbed out the tub, let the water drain away, and
dried herself with the fresh towel Gus had left out for her. She took
the trouble to rub some of her favorite coconut-butter moisture lotion
into her skin and used her regular products on her face. Draped in the
towel, she ran across to her room and considered what to wear. The
guys were making a big effort to make her feel special. She ought to
return the favor.

She pulled out her one and only dress—a simple little black job,
with a high neck, no sleeves, and a tight skirt that finished just above

her knees. She added black stockings and shoes with four-inch heels. She brushed her hair out until it crinkled and secured it on top of her head with a clip. A dab of mascara, a slash of lip gloss, and she was good to go. She examined her reflection and nodded. That was about as good as it got.

"Wish me luck," she said to the kittens as she made her way back to the great room.

* * * *

"What's up, buddy?" Harley asked Fergal as they prepared the fire together.

"She wasn't honest with us about her relationship with Greg." Fergal curled his lip. "They had dinner together recently."

"So what?" Gus asked from the kitchen. "She said they were friends again. Don't mean they're lovers."

"If they were, she wouldn't play with us," Harley said. "She's not the type."

"Still, she lied."

Harley shook his head. "Lighten up and give her a break. I know how you feel about that sort of shit, but I don't think she did actually lie."

"There's an easy enough way to find out," Gus said. "Ask her and clear the air. Then perhaps we can get down to the main event."

Harley sensed a presence behind them, straightened up, and whistled. "Hey, where's Briana?"

Fergal followed the direction of Harley's gaze and did a double take. He'd always known she would scrub up well, just not quite this well. Those legs, encased in thin nylon, went on forever. The dress was classy and sexy at the same time, showcasing her fabulous tits. Fergal's fingers itched to caress them but, damn it, she'd lied! Her expression of studied nonchalance didn't fool him. She was nervous, cared about what they thought of her, and was trying hard not to show it. Was she also playing them, though? That was the question that plagued him.

"You look sensational." Fergal wanted to remain detached but still took her hand, turned it over, and applied his lips to the pulse point inside her wrist.

"I feel overdressed," she said.

"That we can do something about," Gus assured her, winking.

"Come and have a drink."

Harley handed her one of her grandmother's delicate champagne flutes filled with fizzy pink wine and a half strawberry. The three of them picked up their own glasses, and they clinked.

"To pleasure," Gus said.

"Pleasure," they agreed, taking sips.

"Hmm, lovely, it's ages since I had champagne," she said, sneezing when the bubbles went up her nose. "I didn't have you guys pegged as the champagne type."

"When the occasion calls for it," Gus said. "We're pretty adaptable."

Fergal hadn't said a word since greeting her, and he could see his attitude was confusing her almost as much as it confused him. It shouldn't matter that she wasn't being straight with them. Everyone had stuff they didn't choose to share. Even so, he couldn't shake the incident with Greg from his head. He hadn't known Fergal and his buddies were within earshot when he spoke to Briana, his words making it pretty clear that he thought they were an item. Was Briana using the three of them to keep Greg on his toes? She didn't seem the type to play those sorts of games, but Fergal knew better than most that women were capable of all sorts of duplicity.

Gus and Harley flirted with her outrageously, but Fergal couldn't bring himself to join in. Briana sent him frequent sideways glances that implied his attitude was casting a blight upon the proceedings. He wasn't being fair to his buddies, or to her. He told himself repeatedly that Briana was just a fling—one in a long line that the three of them had enjoyed and then forgotten about. There was nothing different about her, and if she chose to cheat on her nearest and dearest, so what?

But she was different, that was the problem. Fergal couldn't have said why. All he knew was the thought of her with that slimeball Greg made his gut lurch. Not that Fergal was falling for her, or anything dorky like that. He never made the same mistake twice, but was prepared to go that extra mile for Briana, even if she didn't deserve it.

She laughed aloud at something Gus said to her, throwing her head back, causing her hair to glance across Fergal's shoulder. He leapt to his feet, the walls of the great room suddenly seeming to close in on him. He needed to get his head straight, and he'd never manage it with her so temptingly close, looking so alluring, so damned sexy…Shit, what was wrong with him?

"I'll just be a moment," he said.

Fergal slipped out the front door and leaned against the wall, breathing hard, waiting for common sense to kick in. The cool night air peppered his heated skin as, protected from the elements by the wrap-around porch, he welcomed the opportunity to get his head together. He told himself to accept the way things were without analyzing them to death, wondering why he was letting Briana's behavior get to him. Now he remembered why he never mixed business with pleasure. Not that he'd been remotely tempted in the past, but then he'd never met anyone quite like Briana before.

But she'd lied…she'd lied.

So what, said a little voice inside his head. Everyone lied at some time or another, and she probably thought her private life was none of his damned business. Except that it was, because she'd agreed to get involved with the three of them. Shit, he didn't need these *relationship* complications. He ought to walk away right now, while he still could.

Too late for that.

Fergal glanced up at the sky. The stars were putting on quite a show tonight, and he could clearly make out several of the constellations. That was something city dwellers never got to appreciate because there was too much artificial light in built-up areas. He sniffed the air, sensing that the good weather would soon break. He could smell rain brewing—perhaps a storm—which would match his mood perfectly. He kicked at the wall, moody and unsettled, unsure why he felt so mad at Briana.

* * * *

No one spoke for a while after Fergal went outside. Only the crackling of logs in the grate and Max's gentle snores broke the tense silence. Briana didn't know what had gotten into Fergal, but figured it was probably something she'd done.

"More champagne, honey?" Harley asked.

She shook her head. Champagne was for celebrations, and this no longer felt like a celebratory situation.

"I'd best check up on dinner," Gus said, heading for the kitchen.

"What's wrong with Fergal?" Briana asked Harley. "Is it something I did?"

"No, it's not you." He focused eyes brimming with intelligence on her face. "Fergal has a lot on his mind."

"Don't we all, but...well, if he's had a change of heart about...you know." She inverted her chin. "I know he thinks he's God's gift but, trust me, I'll get over him."

Harley chuckled. "That's good to know."

"Dinner will be five minutes," Gus called.

"Go and get Fergal, babe," Harley said. "I'll open some wine."

Briana wasn't sure she wanted to get Fergal. As far as she was concerned, he could stay outside all night and freeze his ass off. Sulking was an ugly trait, and she had no intention of pandering to him, or trying to talk him around. Still, someone had to do something about him, and Harley has assigned the task to her.

"All right," she said. "Max needs to go out anyway." At the sound of his name, the dog stirred from his position in front of the fire and trotted toward the door. "But if he's still pouting, I warn you, I'll be right back without him."

Harley laughed. "That I'd pay good money to see."

She opened the door and found Fergal leaning against the outside wall of the house, one foot bent up behind him, his expression remote, forbidding. He glanced up when he heard the door open but said nothing. Max, oblivious to the strained atmosphere, dashed past them both and attended to his business.

"Okay," she said patiently. "What's wrong?"

"You lied to me."

"Pardon?" Whatever she'd expected him to say, that certainly wasn't it.

"You said Greg was nothing to you."

"He isn't."

"You had dinner with him."

Briana placed her hands on her hips and scowled up at the angry Adonis holding up her wall, totally unable to understand his anger. "So, that doesn't mean we're joined at the hip."

He didn't say anything for a moment but the condemnation in his eye made her stomach curdle. It also ignited her anger. What right did he have to question her personal life, especially when she knew absolutely nothing about his and didn't attempt to pry?

"Where the hell do you get off, casting moral judgment on my life choices?"

"Ah, so you admit it. The two of you are involved."

"Thank you very much!" Briana was fit to explode with anger. "You think I'd be in a relationship with one man and yet be willing to enter into another with all three of you at once?" She tossed her head and paced the length of the wooden verandah, too angry to remain still. "Well, I guess that tells me all I need to know about your impression of me."

He caught her arm in a viselike grip as she paced past his position. "What else am I supposed to think? He doesn't leave you alone for five minutes, and the two of you seem pretty damned tight."

"Not that it's any of your business, but I owe him."

He rolled his eyes. "Yeah, of course you do."

Briana resisted the temptation to pummel his chest with her fists, but only because it was so damned solid that she'd probably hurt herself rather than him. "He was here for me when I needed him, but I wouldn't expect you to know anything about neighborly behavior."

"You were right about your temper matching your hair color," he said, surprising her by the abrupt switch in his mood. "I look forward to checking that the collars and cuffs match."

"In your dreams! You don't get to talk to me like you just did and then pretend everything's hunky-dory."

"I'm sorry." He shrugged impossibly broad shoulders. She recalled the precise dimensions of those shoulders as they'd looked when he'd spent the day working without his shirt on. She shook her head to dispel the image. She was mad as heck at him and didn't need those sorts of distractions tempering her…well, temper. "I don't know what it is about you, Miss Briana, but you seem able to stir up aspects of my character I'm not proud of."

"Not good enough."

"No, I guess not." He sent her a smoldering smile. "Tell me what Greg did to make you feel so beholden to him."

"I thought you'd already figured it out for yourself," she replied, her voice dripping with sarcasm.

"Look, I'm sorry. Can we start over? Just humor me."

She ought to tell him to go to the devil. Instead, something in his attitude, his hangdog expression, and the haunted look in his eye quelled her anger.

"If you must know, I got back here too late to see my grandmother before she died. She's the only real parent I ever had. How do you think that made me feel?"

"Briana, I—"

"You wanted to hear this, so shut up and listen. I had no idea Gran was so ill. She made everyone I keep in touch with promise not to tell." Briana felt tears welling but willed them away. She was angry with this jerk, not upset. "She didn't want me to see her the way she was at the end, and so I never got to say good-bye."

"Shit, Briana." He loosened his grip on her arm but didn't release her. "That must have been tough."

"You have no idea, because you have no heart."

"That's not precisely true."

"I was alone, and upset, and Greg kept me company. He did all the horrible things that I didn't want to face, like talking to the funeral parlor and, well...I appreciated it. He was a good friend when I needed one. Besides, I didn't want to be alone."

"So he kept you warm and cozy at night?"

"You really are a piece of work." She gave him the benefit of her best assault glare. "It's not that way with us. He wants it to be, but I don't. There's no pizzazz between us, nothing to tempt me to look upon him as anything more than a friend." She pulled out of his grasp and folded her arms across her chest. It was chilly out here, but she was so riled up that she barely felt the cold on her bare arms. "There won't be anything between us, either. You've spoiled what I thought might be a fun encounter with your possessive jealousy."

"I'm sorry, babe—"

"Besides, you know just about everything there is to know about my life, but I know diddly-squat about yours because you haven't seen fit to share, and I'm too nice to probe."

He moved so fast that she didn't realize what he intended to do until it was too late to stop him. Suddenly he wasn't the one leaning against the wall anymore, but she was. He placed one hand on either side of her head and braced his arms. A few inches of space separated their bodies as his handsome face loomed over hers. Even so, she felt his vital heat searing into her and found it difficult to maintain her anger.

"Let me go," she said, trying to duck beneath his arm. "I'm pissed with you."

"You have every right to be." He shook his head, sending hair cascading across his eyes. "I've behaved like a jackass."

She bit back a smile. "No arguments there. Wanna tell me why?"

He was quiet for so long that when he finally spoke it took her by surprise. His voice was pure liquid venom, and the bitterness in his expression made her shiver.

"I was married in a previous life," he said.

"Oh." It hadn't occurred to Briana to ask if any of them were married. She'd just assumed that they weren't. "You say *was*. What happened?"

"She was the love of my life, and I was the happiest man on earth, especially when she told me we were going to start a family." He grimaced. "I've always wanted kids."

"Were you in the marines at the time?"

"Yes, but mostly based Stateside so we didn't have to be apart that often. Our daughter was born three years ago next month." A flicker of a smile broke through his granite expression. "Needless to say, she was *the* most beautiful, the most perfect baby in the world."

"I'm sure you make a fine dad."

"That's what I once thought, too."

He fell into a sullen silence, and although she was burning with curiosity, Briana sensed it would be better not to prompt him. Whatever he had to say, he clearly didn't enjoy talking about it. She only hoped the baby hadn't died, but that's what she assumed, because he spoke about parenthood in the past tense.

"When she was a year old, my daughter got sick and needed a blood transfusion. Turned out she has a rare blood group." He paused for what seemed like forever, scowling at a point above her head. "And you know what's so damned amusing? Neither Sheila nor I shared that group. Nor could we produce a child who did."

"Oh, no. That's terrible." Instinctively Briana lifted one hand and gently traced the line of his cheek, smoothing away the anger lines at the side of his mouth, wishing she could erase the hurt she saw reflected in his eyes as easily. "She'd cheated on you."

"I guess you could say that." The concentrated fury in his expression stole Briana's breath away. "And when she was caught out, she tried to put the blame on me, saying she got lonely when I was away."

"Did she know the baby wasn't yours?"

"No, how could she? I guess she just hoped."

"Did the little girl recover?"

"Yeah, her *real* daddy did just about the only thing he's ever done for her and gave blood."

"No wonder you can't stand people lying to you."

"Still, I shouldn't have reacted the way I did."

"Presumably you divorced."

"We sure did, but I still support her and our little girl."

"Even though she isn't yours?"

"Her real dad took a hike when the shit hit the fan. Someone has to take care of them."

"Not all men would be so understanding," she said softly, conscious of the storm leaving eyes that had become dark and intense. His lips hovered a whisper away from her own, and she breathed in the essence of him—a combination of sandalwood soap, anger, and hot, desirable male. "Do you still see your wife and daughter?"

"Oh yeah, every time the three of us make a tour of our families." He paused. "My ex is Gus's sister."

Chapter Nine

"You're the only person I've ever spoken to about it," Fergal said.

"Has it made you feel better?"

"Nope, but this will."

He lowered his head and captured her lips in a deep, demanding kiss. Fire lanced through his veins when she parted her lips and allowed him to invade her mouth with his tongue. She tasted of champagne, strawberries, and the outdoors. She tasted like heaven. His arms closed possessively around her body as he crushed it against his own—her soft curves a thrilling contrast to the solid planes of his chest. He lazily explored the contours of her mouth, their tongues tangling in an exotic dance that set his cock throbbing and his pulse racing at twice its normal rate.

If they carried on like this, he'd have to take her, right here, right now, on the verandah. He couldn't remember the last time he'd been so hard, so desperate to sink his dick into a warm, tight pussy. Her warm, tight pussy. That wouldn't be fair to the others, so he reluctantly broke the kiss.

"I've wanted to do that since the first moment I set eyes on you," he said softly. "I'm real sorry that I behaved so badly."

She kissed the end of his nose, her eyes muddy with passion. "You're forgiven, but just so you know, this is a no-strings-attached thing. I don't do emotional attachment."

"Me neither, not anymore."

"Good."

"Any more conditions you wanna lay out?" Fergal asked, running his fingers down the length of her spine until his hands came to rest on her pert ass.

"Nothing springs to mind at this particular moment."

"Then I guess we'd best go join the others."

"How come you're still such good buddies with Gus, after what his sister did to you?"

"It's not his fault. He was mortified when he found out she'd been mixing more than just soufflés with one of the chefs in their dad's restaurants. So was the rest of her family. I don't have any close relations of my own, so Gus's lot kinda adopted me when Gus and I first joined the marines and got friendly. I spent most of my leaves at their place in Chicago, especially when Sheila and I started dating."

"And where's Sheila and your daughter now?"

"They moved to Florida, but always seem to be in Chicago whenever we are. Funny that. Anyway, it's good to see my little girl, but I try to avoid Sheila."

"Because she wants you back?"

How the hell does she know that? "Perhaps, but it ain't gonna happen."

The door opened just as Fergal pulled her into his arms again.

"I hate to interrupt," Harley said, "but Gus says you're to come right now or the food goes in the trash. You know how he gets when he's got his chef's hat on."

Fergal rolled his eyes. "Don't I ever."

He laced his fingers with Briana's, and all three of them returned to the great room, just behind Max, who'd obviously seen the door open and smelled the food. Gus looked relieved when he saw Fergal and Briana walk in, hand in hand.

"You guys need to sit down right now," he said.

"Briana's overdressed," Fergal said as she was about to slide into the seat that Harley held out for her.

"I'm what?"

"Remember what we told you last night," Fergal replied, sending her a curling smile. "Our games don't start in the bedroom, sweetheart. They start when I say they do."

"Who put you in charge?" she demanded.

"He's the boss," Harley replied quietly. "Don't fight him, Briana. Just do as he says."

Fergal watched carefully for her reaction to Harley's words, wondering if they were taking her too far, too fast. She'd been pretty angry outside, and he wasn't sure if she was completely over it yet. *Come on, darlin', you know you want to.* When she moistened her lips with the tip of her tongue and met his gaze with one of reckless sensuality, he wanted to punch the air in jubilation.

"Take your dress off," he said.

"What! You want me to sit at the table in my underclothes?"

"Darlin', if I decide it's appropriate, you'll sit at the table in the nude."

Her eyes sparkled, her face colored, all vestiges of anger replaced by intense anticipation. "All right, but I need to—"

"That would be all right, Master, or all right, Sir," Fergal corrected, taking a seat directly opposite the one that Briana would soon occupy. "Whenever one of us speaks to you, you will respond with respect. Do you understand?"

"Yes, Master." She turned her back toward Harley. "Would you help me with my zipper please, Sir?"

Harley sent Fergal and Gus a triumphant look over Briana's head as he yanked down her zipper and Briana stepped out of her dress. All three men inhaled sharply. She was wearing a near-transparent black bra, edged with red and yellow flowers, with matching panties and garter belt. She blushed deeply as she absorbed their scrutiny, but Fergal could tell she'd already gotten over her embarrassment and had to be enjoying the looks of appreciation they made no effort to conceal. Her legs were fantastic, her butt small and pert, her tits as ripe and plump as Fergal had hoped they would be. He could see dark nipples and pebbled areolas pressing against her bra. And as for those freckles, Fergal planned to spend hours joining up the dots with his finger. Or perhaps something a little sexier.

Briana made to sit down, but Fergal slapped his hand on the table, causing her to jump.

"No one told you to move."

"Sorry, Master."

"You may sit down, Briana."

When she did so and Harley had pushed her chair in for her, her tits formed a ledge that could easily rest on the edge of the table. Shit, how long could he hold out before getting his hands on them?

"Place your hands behind the back of your chair, Briana," he said.

As soon as she did so, Harley cuffed them in place. It pushed her tits out even more, obliging Fergal to suppress a groan. He was supposed to be the one in control here, but, fuck it, it was hard—quite literally—to remain in that role.

"Hey, how can I eat if—"

"No one gave you permission to speak."

"I have to have permission to say something?"

"Pardon?"

She swallowed. "I have to have permission to say something, Master?"

"Absolutely. You also keep your eyes lowered, unless we tell you to do otherwise. As for eating, Harley and Gus will feed you."

Gus cut the Spanish *tortilla* he'd made as an appetizer into small squares, speared one piece with his fork and placed it against her lips. She disobeyed Fergal's last order by fastening her gaze on his face as she parted her lips and swallowed down the food. Fergal locked gazes with her as he cut up his own food and took a bite. She moistened her lips with the tip of her tongue and continued to defy him by holding his gaze.

"Is your cunt wet, Briana?" he asked.

"Yes, Master."

"Get a towel, Harley. We don't want her ruining a perfectly good chair because she can't control her desires."

Harley grinned. "I'll be right back."

Gus lifted her wineglass and placed it to her lips. He tilted it as she drank and a little wine trickled down her chin.

"Leave it," Fergal said when Gus made to wipe it away.

Harley returned with the towel, and Briana lifted first one buttock and then the other so he could place it beneath her. Then all three men watched in fascination as the red wine trickled down her chin, landing on her breast bone. Gus leaned forward and licked it away, slowly. Briana gasped but remembered not to speak.

"Did either of your lovers ever clamp your nipples?" Fergal asked as the meal continued.

"No, Master. Why would they?"

"You'll find out."

They'd finished the entrée, and Gus cleared away the plates. He returned a short time later with a dish oozing fresh cream and fruit.

"We'll have dessert in front of the fire," Fergal said, standing up.

"I couldn't eat another thing," Briana said. "Master," she added hastily.

"You'll do as you're told," Fergal replied, fixing her with a stern gaze.

Harley released Briana's hands and helped her to her feet. She walked slowly toward the great room, and Fergal, directly behind her, grinned when he saw her honey trickling down the insides of her thighs. She was turned on, ready to play. They wouldn't have any trouble getting her to agree to what he had in mind for her next.

* * * *

Briana felt detached from what was happening to her. It couldn't possibly be her, parading about in her underwear in front of three men who appeared to like what they saw. No one had fallen about laughing when they saw her belly, her pendulous tits, or her ugly knees. They didn't even seem to mind her freckles, possibly because she still had *some* clothing to hide behind. If, when, they removed her bra and her tits fell down to her knees, they were bound to come to their senses and tell her they'd made a mistake.

Briana was starting to get impatient with them. This looking business was all very well, but none of them had touched her yet, and Briana was desperate to be touched, if only for reassurance. She gasped when she reached the fire. In front of it was a huge comforter, large enough for them all to occupy it. Was that what Fergal had in mind?

Before she could decide, she felt his firm body pressing against her back as his large hands moved around to cup her breasts and his rigid cock pressed into her ass. He tweaked the nipples hard enough to make her gasp as he weighed her hated appendages in his hands.

"Very nice," he purred in her ear.

He likes them?

Briana opened her mouth to tell him that he didn't need to pay her false compliments. She was well aware of her physical shortcomings. Then she remembered she wasn't allowed to speak unless spoken to and closed her mouth again. She felt Fergal fumble with the clasp and her bra fell away. He threw it on the floor and caught her breasts as they tumbled free, rubbing and massaging them with sweeps of his capable hands while nibbling at her shoulder blade and sending delicious thrills sliding through her.

Heavens, someone had unfastened one of her stockings and rolled it slowly down her leg, turning the simple task into something that was sensuous beyond her imagination. It made her feel feminine, desirable and *slim.* The pulsating ache throbbing through her sensitized body sent a vortex of desire shooting straight to her pussy. She'd never known anything quite like it. If anyone so much as touched her sopping cunt then she'd probably come then and there, such was the strength of her desperation.

As though reading her mind, one of the guys slid his hand inside her panties and rubbed his palm teasingly across her mons. Briana moaned. Having three men touching her, exploring her, teasing her, was beyond anything she'd imagined feasible. Pulsating warmth tumbled through her, shards of pleasure blasting her body from all sides as Fergal dropped a sizzling line of damp kisses across her shoulders and continued to play with her tits. Her other stocking disappeared, along with her garter belt. Her panties fell around her ankles, and she was now completely naked.

"She's ready," Harley said.

"Lie down, Briana," Fergal said. "This way, with your head closest to the fire. Lift your arms above your head. Harley's gonna fasten them to the guard rail."

"Oh." She scrambled into position, glad that the only illumination in the room was provided by the fire and candlelight. Perhaps they hadn't been able to see her well enough to notice the flaws. She was glad to delay the inevitable.

"Not oh," Fergal said sharply, tapping her thigh. "You have to earn this. Ask Harley to cuff your wrists."

"Please, Master Harley," she said, biting her lower lip to stop herself from laughing or, worse, from her excitement becoming too evident. "Would you fasten my hands to the rail, please?"

"You got it, babe."

Gus carefully placed his creamy dessert on a nearby side table, which is when Briana realized what they had planned. They hadn't brought any plates from the dining room because they planned to use her body as a serving station. Her already sopping cunt leaked a little more and her nipples beaded. *Bring it on, boys!*

All three men removed their shirts but kept the rest of their clothing in place. She wanted to object but already knew better. It was a real turn-on being at their mercy and only being allowed to speak when spoken to. If they wanted to give her pleasure with their mouths and tongues before she got to see them as nature intended, who was she to complain?

She feasted her eyes on their gorgeous chests, wishing she could photograph them again at such close quarters. Gus took a large spoonful of cream and dropped it onto one nipple, sending all thoughts of photography out of her mind. Harley did the same with the opposite one. Together they bent their heads and feasted on her tits, sending Briana's body into sensory overload. They sucked and nipped, their hands kneading the ample flesh almost savagely. At first it hurt and she tensed up.

"Relax into it, honey," Gus raised his head to say. "Let the pain work for you."

Oh really? Well, she'd try anything once. Briana forced herself to breathe deeply and placed her trust in them. Astonishingly the pain gradually became pleasurable, and she gasped with surprise.

"See," Gus said in a smug tone.

"She's a fast learner," Fergal agreed.

She couldn't see where Fergal actually was since he'd abandoned her shoulders. His voice came from the vicinity of her feet. It sounded as though he approved, and she was ridiculously glad to have pleased him. Something flashed, causing her to jump against her cuffed hands. When her vision cleared she realized that Fergal had used her camera to photograph her in the nude, being used as a dining table by two randy hunks.

"Seems only fair, Briana. You photographed us without our permission, which, incidentally, will earn you a spanking later on."

"Yes, Master," she said, getting into the way of things and having a ball. "I was wrong and must be punished."

"Christ!" Harley said.

"Bring your knees up and spread your legs wide," Fergal ordered.

As soon as she'd done so, acutely aware that her cunt would now be open to them and on clear view, the camera flashed again. Several times. Well, if they thought her pussy was worthy of being recorded for posterity, that was fine by her.

She heard the camera being placed on a table and became aware of a large presence crouching between her legs, blowing softly on her clit. She gasped, only just managing not to elevate her body in her desperation to have the lips that were doing the blowing a lot closer. Was Fergal finally going to fuck her? It had to be him. She could see Gus's dark-blond hair flopping over one of her tits and Harley's light-brown crowning glory making itself at home on her opposite side. Her pussy lips were pulled apart and something cool was smeared over her pubic bone. *Oh my, cream!* More was pushed inside her. Then her legs were lifted and thrown over a pair of wide shoulders.

She felt more cream being rubbed into her midriff and lips and teeth assiduously removing it. Fergal's lips latched onto her pussy, and she cried out, pushing her hips into his mouth. He immediately withdrew, and she protested with a cry of disappointment. She really liked his mouth. She especially liked what he'd been doing with his tongue, and she definitely didn't want it to stop.

"Keep absolutely still, Briana," Fergal said. "If you move your hips again, we'll send you to bed. Alone." *They wouldn't?* "Do you understand?"

It appeared they would. Either way, Briana wasn't prepared to risk it. "Yes, Master Fergal."

"Good girl. Now keep still and let me eat my dessert. I've got a terrible hunger to satisfy."

That makes two of us.

When Fergal reapplied his lips to her vagina, Briana felt she'd died and gone to heaven. Expertly he whirled his tongue across her clit, making it almost impossible not to push herself deeper into his mouth. Red-hot heat whipped through her bloodstream when he transferred his attention off her pussy and sucked the fruit and cream from inside her. She never would have imagined such delicious torture possible. Her internal muscles coiled and strained, endeavoring to draw him deeper. He wasn't buying it and refused to be rushed. Harley bit hard on her nipple, and she cried out because it felt so wonderful it was impossible not to react verbally. Who would have thought she'd ever enjoy pain?

"Hell," Fergal said. "Some of that cream's gone too deep. What can we do about that?"

She figured he expected her to answer, even though he hadn't given her permission to speak. She bit back a laugh and clamped her lips together. Playing him at his own game was fun.

"Only one thing for it."

Her heart rate accelerated when she heard his pants hit the ground and foil ripping. *Please God, make that a condom.* Her wish was granted when the head of his enormous erection nudged at her pussy lips. Hell, it was too big. She could tell that much without even seeing it. She should have warned them that she was small down there. Not that Fergal seemed too bothered. He inched his way inside her, groaning himself now and not sounding nearly so controlled as he made himself out to be.

"Geez, darlin', it's a tight fit. Am I hurting you?"

"No, Master Fergal, it feels real good. But I'm very small."

He chuckled. "No, you're not, sweet thing. You just haven't been fucked by a real man for a while. Probably not ever, but all that's about to change."

Gus and Harley removed themselves from her tits. Someone threw a couple of cushions beneath her butt, and Fergal drove himself a little deeper, stretching the walls of her pussy beyond anything that she would have imagined possible. Filling her so completely that her sheath spasmed. If she was allowed to talk, she'd ask Fergal to carry on giving her head. She desperately needed to come, and it would never happen this way. Not that it mattered. She could always bring herself off later. The only important thing was to give Fergal pleasure. And the other two as well, if they wanted her. Gus was still kneeling to one side of her, out of Fergal's range as he braced his weight on his arms and drove himself a little deeper still. She heard cream squelch out of her. She could see the extent of Gus's excitement in the periphery of her vision and knew that he at least wanted her very much indeed. He caught her watching, grabbed his rigid cock in both his hands and grinned at her.

"See what you've done to me, sugar?"

"Fergal! You're splitting me in two."

"I'm hurting you?"

"Hell no. I just didn't think it would be possible for you to—"

"Shush. No talking. You've got almost all of me now."

Briana widened her eyes, forgetting she wasn't supposed to talk. "There's more?"

"Another inch or so." He eased himself deeper and sighed. "That's it, babe, you've got everything I can give you. You feel that? You can talk, Briana. How does it make you feel?"

"Complete," she said succinctly. "I had no idea."

"You can move now, darlin'. Let's do this together."

"Thank you, Master Fergal."

"That's it, honey," Harley's gravelly voice said. "Ride Fergal's big cock. I just bet you love having him buried deep inside your cunt, don't you, babe?"

"Yes, Master Harley." She gritted her teeth, perspiration peppering her brow as she moved in tight formation with Harley, pushing her hips forward to welcome his deep thrusts. "It's heavenly."

"Aw, don't tell him he's angelic," Gus said. "We'll never hear the end of it."

"Sorry, Master Gus."

Briana panted as liquid heat coursed through her veins. Funny, she felt the tingling she always got just before she climaxed, but climaxing through penetration simply didn't work for her.

"It's okay, little Briana," Gus said, still massaging his erection. He and Harley must have shed their clothes at the same time Fergal did.

It was hard to keep track. "When Fergal has finished with you, I've got just the thing for your dessert." He waggled his cock close to her face. "Can't wait to see your sweet lips wrapped around this baby."

Harley increased the rate and angle of his thrusts, and her body responded like it had developed a mind of its own.

"Fergal, I think...I don't believe it." She widened her eyes and their gazes collided. "I've never been able to—"

"Just ride it, darlin'. Take what you need from me."

Briana's world spun out of control as she thrashed her head from side to side. One of the guys pinched a nipple as the most mind-blowing orgasm hit, short-circuiting her bloodstream and sending her toppling over the edge. Pleasure spangled through her entire system, harder, deeper, more intensely than anything she'd ever managed alone. And it seemed to go on indefinitely. She opened her eyes and was blown away by the expression of deep satisfaction in Fergal's glowing eyes, even as the muscles in his arms trembled and she could tell he was having a hard time holding back until she was done.

Finally her own pulsating ceased, which was when Fergal picked up the pace again. His laden balls crashed against her buttocks, and his labored breathing peppered her face.

"That's it, darlin'," he said. "Now we're really fucking. I'm so deep inside you, Briana, that it feels like I've died and gone to heaven."

She moved smoothly with him as she sensed his cock thicken and fill. Suddenly she was acutely aware of the power of her femininity because, after all, it was her who'd caused him to abandon what she suspected was normally rigid self-control.

"Shit, darlin', I hope you're ready."

Me, ready? I've already come.

He wasn't to know that once was more than she'd dared to hope for. It was time to bring her acting skills into play. Astonishingly, that proved to be unnecessary because his pleasure communicated itself to her and she felt another orgasm building. This simply couldn't be happening.

But it was and Briana wasn't about to waste time wondering how. She already knew why. Having all three of them tending to her needs had well and truly blown away the hang-ups about sex she'd never really acknowledged but had probably always known were there. She bit her lip to suppress a triumphant smile, aware that any prudish tendencies she might have possessed had been well and truly…well, laid.

"Fergal, I—"

"I'm gonna come, darlin'. So are you. I can feel you closing around my cock."

He thrust into her so hard that she was barely able to hold her position. They cried out together as Fergal's thick length pulsated inside her and she felt him shoot his load into the condom. Her own world shattered for a second time in five minutes as their creative energy and the physical alchemy that existed between them drove her out of her mind.

They collapsed in a heap of sweat, cream, and laughter afterward. Someone released her hands, someone else kissed her lips. She and Fergal struggled to regain their breath.

"Why didn't you tell me you've never come through penetration before?" Fergal asked.

Chapter Ten

Briana blinked up at Fergal, her expression dumbfounded. "How could you possibly know that?"

It was Gus who answered her. "We could tell from your reaction. You didn't expect Fergal to be able to satisfy you, did you, honey?"

"Well, no, but a lot of women live perfectly happy lives without being sexually fulfilled. It wouldn't have mattered."

"The hell it wouldn't," Fergal replied.

"You have a lot to feel responsible for," she told him. "What you've never had you never miss, but now—"

"Don't worry," Fergal said, running a finger lazily over her belly. "There's plenty more where that came from."

"Don't look at me. I'm fat!"

"You are not fat!" three voices protested in unison.

"I am. My tits are too big, my belly sticks out, and—"

"Don't ever let us hear you put yourself down like that again," Fergal said sternly.

"Why not? It's true."

"Some bastard's really played a number with your self-confidence," Gus said, scowling. "Hasn't it occurred to you yet that you turn heads everywhere you go, for all the right reasons?"

"No." She shook her head, obviously having no idea just how desirable her voluptuous curves made her. "It's not fashionable to have tits."

Harley laughed. "Ask a man, any man, for his opinion on that subject."

"The only part of me that I thought looked okay was my ass. Now people pay to have their buttocks enlarged." She shook her head. "Why would anyone pay to have a backside that resembles a shelf?"

"You got me there, babe. And just so that you know, your ass is absolutely fine just the way it is." Gus took her hand and pulled her to her feet. "Come on, let's get you cleaned up." Gus swept her into his arms and headed for the bathroom, the other two following behind. "Seems to me we need to deal with your negative body image issues and teach you a bit more about your passionate nature."

"You don't have that much time."

"We'll make time," Harley said, setting the water running in the spacious shower stall and ushering them all inside. "We were sent here to make sure you didn't have problems you couldn't handle. Seems to me you have a whole ton of them, just not the ones we thought we'd come here to fix."

"Is it big enough for all of us?" Briana asked when she found herself squeezed between their bodies.

"If we get up close and personal," Gus replied with a wicked grin.

They washed her all over, including her hair, because they'd gotten a bit carried away with the cream, and she was now a delightful, sticky mess.

"Got to concentrate on the important places," Gus told her as he wiped her pussy repeatedly with a washcloth. "You sore, honey?"

She shook her head. "Not in the least."

"That's good to know, 'cause I gotta tell you, watching Fergal fuck you was a real turn-on for Harley and me."

She sent him a sultry smile and touched his cheek. "Well, we can't have you guys being uncomfortable, can we now?"

"Wouldn't be nice," Harley agreed with a lascivious smirk, patting her ass.

Fergal shut the water off and exited the stall first. He held out a large towel and wrapped Briana in it when she stepped out. Between them they dried her off. Harley toweled her hair and brushed it free of tangles. Satisfied that she was clean and comfortable, Gus nodded to the others.

"Time for her second lesson," he said, scooping her into his arms again. "Come on, darlin', let's go and make ourselves cozy."

In her bedroom Fergal took a chair in the corner, but Gus didn't fool himself into believing that he or Harley would be in charge. Fergal was their natural leader, and not just because he'd outranked them in the service. Some people were born to lead, and Fergal just happened to be one of them. He and Harley were cool about it since Fergal had proved himself to be a loyal comrade and friend times without number. He was no dictator, either. If Gus or Harley disagreed with one of his decisions, they weren't afraid to say so. Fergal always listened, taking on board their opinions and often changing his mind as a consequence.

When it came to sharing women, they were all on the same page. They enjoyed the same things, had yet to fall out over any female, and no female had come between them. *Well, not since...no, don't go there.* This particular situation was unlike anything they'd handled before. Before Gus had even had a taste of Briana for himself he had a hard time imagining them walking away from her. She was special. Gus couldn't have said why. They'd been with more beautiful women. They'd been with women who were way more experienced, but there was just something about Briana that got to him. Her tough exterior hid a touching vulnerability and a whole raft of self-doubt that any man would go that extra mile to fix.

"Get her on her hands and knees." Fergal's voice broke through Gus's reverie. "She needs to be punished for speaking out of turn before you guys take things any farther."

"You heard the man," Gus said to Briana. "Get on your hands and knees for us, darlin', and ask Fergal to punish you."

Her eyes sparkled with anticipation as she scrambled into position. All three guys sucked in breaths when her large tits dangled so invitingly beneath her, but made no comment about them. Fergal left her where she was for a while, not speaking, making her wait. Her pussy was leaking again. This chick was one hot property. No, not chick, Gus mentally amended. She was definitely special. He'd thought so the moment he'd laid eyes on her, and Fergal definitely did as well. Why else had he gotten so hot under the collar when he thought she'd lied to them? Gus didn't know what had passed between them when they'd been outside for so long, but he was glad to see some life come back to Fergal's eye. It had disappeared when Gus's bitch of a sister did the dirty on him, and although Fergal insisted none of the blame lay with Gus, somehow he'd always felt responsible. He'd introduced them, knowing how his sister liked to operate, and should have tried harder to warn Fergal.

Eventually Fergal uncoiled his tall frame and strolled toward the bed. He was erect again. They all were. They'd have to be eunuchs not to be aroused by the sight of Briana on her hands and knees, cute butt just crying out to be spanked, honey trickling down her thighs, huge nipples begging to be bitten. It wasn't the sort of sight a man got to see every day. Far as Gus was concerned, he'd never seen anything quite as mind-blowingly sensuous ever before.

"We need a safe word, Briana," he said. "If we do something you don't like, or if you want us to stop for any reason, say the safe word. What word would you like to use?"

"Pollution," she said without hesitation. "I'm an environmentalist and pollution is definitely the enemy. I won't forget that one."

"Fair enough. Pollution it is."

Fergal laid one large hand on her butt and then bent his head to kiss each cheek. Briana inhaled sharply but didn't speak. She was definitely a fast learner. Fergal's index finger ran lazily down the crack in her butt, stopping to circle her anus for a second or two. She tensed up, and Gus assumed she'd never had anal sex before. Good. If they could persuade her to give it a try, it would be a privilege to show her what she'd been missing.

Without warning her to expect it, Fergal laid a sharp slap across her buttocks. This time she did cry out, but gamely held her position.

"Breathe deeply and concentrate on the pain," Fergal said in a soft, hypnotic voice.

"Yes, Master."

He slapped her again, a little harder this time. And then a third time. Her ass was now delightfully pink, her limbs trembled, and she was perspiring.

"How does it feel?" Fergal asked.

"I don't think it was hard enough," she replied, peeping up at them from beneath the curtain of her rapidly-drying hair. "I was really disobedient and deserve to be punished harder, Masters."

All three of them laughed. It would have been impossible, at least from Gus's perspective, to do otherwise.

"Oh, we'll punish you a damned sight harder than this, once you get used to it," Fergal told her, his deep, rich voice a whispered promise. "We'll use paddles, floggers, perhaps even whips." He bent his head and kissed her buttocks again, then stood and rubbed the crack in her ass with the tip of his cock. "You can count on it. Now, what do you have to say?"

"Thank you for punishing me, Master Fergal."

Without another word, Fergal went back to his chair and sat down, one foot propped on his opposite thigh, still rigidly erect. This was Harley and Gus's cue to have some fun and neither man hesitated.

"Turn over and lie on your back, darlin'," Gus said.

As soon as she'd done so, Gus straddled her body and leaned in for a deep, drugging kiss. She responded with sweet enthusiasm, and he savored the treat of her mouth as his tongue explored and he deepened the kiss. He wanted to make this last forever, but his needs were too urgent. He'd have her suck his cock in a minute, but first Gus slithered down her body and paid homage to her gorgeous tits. How could she possibly think they were too large? Somebody had made a sport out of putting her down. Whoever that bastard was, Gus would like to throttle him.

Briana squirmed beneath him and buried her fingers in his hair, sighing as he bit one of her solidified nipples.

"Like that, do you, sugar?"

"Yes, Master Gus. It feels wonderful."

He slid one hand down to her pussy, smiling at her wetness. When a couple of his fingers invaded her slick warmth, she cried out and thrust her hips against them.

"Keep still, Briana."

"Sorry, Master Gus. I forgot."

"I could use some help here," Gus said to Harley. "I don't reckon I'm enough for our little Briana. She needs two men at once to keep her happy."

"Looks that way," Harley agreed, sliding onto the bed.

Gus ceded his place on top of her and told Briana to get back on her hands and knees. Once she did so, he slipped into position sideways beneath her, his cock right in line with her sweet lips.

"Suck it for me, babe," he said in a husky voice.

Briana exceeded his expectations by removing one hand from where it was supporting her weight and using it to squeeze his balls. She exerted just enough pressure to make him moan. At the same time she sucked his head into her mouth and sipped at his arousal.

"That's it, darlin'," Harley's voice said. "You let Gus fuck your face while I fuck your sweet pussy. We're gonna prove to you that Fergal ain't the only one capable of rocking your world."

Her teeth nipped painfully at Gus's cock, presumably because Harley had suited up and entered her. Gus didn't know and was beyond caring. All he was concerned about was the pressure of her skilled lips and the progress of her tongue as she licked him from tip to balls and then back again. Shit, she was way too good at this. He wouldn't last two minutes at this rate. Gus tried to think about the starving millions in Africa, dead cats, all the stuff that men were supposed to think about to prevent themselves from coming too soon.

It didn't help much.

A loud slap sounded in the otherwise quiet room, presumably because Harley had rapped her ass. She made a strangled sound around his cock, and Gus was aware of a spurt of jism shooting from it. The camera flashed. Presumably Fergal was recording the scene, and Gus would enjoy seeing the results. He reached for one of her tits, pulled her nipple as far away from her body as the skin would stretch, and pinched it hard, just as Harley spanked her butt for a second time. She almost chocked on his cock but gamely kept sucking.

"That's is, babe," Harley grunted. "You've got it all now. I bet you're just loving this?"

"She can't answer you, Harley." Fergal sounded amused. "Her mouth is completely full of Gus's cock."

"It'll soon be full of Gus's sperm." Gus's voice was a desperate moan as he struggled to hold back the surging tide of his orgasm. "I can't last much longer."

"Discipline, Dalton," Fergal said, chuckling. "Discipline."

"I don't remember you lasting too long, Captain," Gus replied, panting as his balls tightened and he felt the rushing excitement surge through his veins. "That's it, darlin', open your throat for me. I'm gonna shoot my load. Shit, here it comes!"

Gus's cock pulsated inside her mouth as his sperm gushed deep into the back of her throat. There was so much of it that she could barely swallow fast enough, but she did one hell of a job trying.

"Ah, sweetheart," he said, slipping out of her mouth and covering her slick lips with his own. "You're something else."

Her eyes glistened with passion as Harley continued to pummel her cunt. Briana's body spasmed, and she cried out as she pushed back against him.

"Please, Master Harley," she sobbed. "I can't wait any longer."

"It's okay, darlin', take what you need."

Harley slapped her backside and barely waited for her tremors to subside before he upped the pace of his thrusts, driving himself into her hard and fast. Gus played with her tits, wondering if she'd manage a second orgasm before Harley ejaculated. Her eyes opened very wide and she screamed loud enough to wake the dead as Harley came hard and Briana obviously did, too.

All three of them fell onto the bed, laughing, panting, totally spent. Gus made brief eye contact with Harley and could see he'd been as astonished as Gus himself was by what she'd just done for them. Their little Briana, who'd led a sheltered life and claimed not to be very experienced in the sack, sure was a natural sub.

"You okay, sweetheart?" he asked, leaning up on one elbow to kiss her.

"Wonderful," she replied, looking totally dazed. "What have you guys done to me?"

Gus wanted to ask the same question of her.

Chapter Eleven

"You okay, darlin'?" Fergal asked as he cleaned Briana up with a cloth he'd just collected from the bathroom.

"Absolutely fine." She stretched, sharing a smug, satiated smile between the three of them. "I still can't believe what you guys have done for me. I was absolutely convinced I couldn't orgasm through penetration."

"Now you know different." Fergal pulled back the covers. "Come on, honey, into bed with you."

"Oh, but I thought—" She glanced at Fergal's cock, which was still half-erect.

"Hey, don't be greedy." He tapped her arm. "You've had all you can take from us first time around."

She glared at him. "Isn't that for me to decide?"

"Haven't you remembered anything we just taught you?" Fergal wagged a finger beneath her nose. "We get to call the shots. Your only requirement is to enjoy yourself."

"Yes, but won't you be uncomfortable?"

Fergal's cock refused to subside, and he was pretty damned sure that situation would continue until he put distance between them. Just looking at her lush body and come-hither smile made him want to...Hell, she was a fucking witch! "I'll live," he said curtly.

"Can I ask you some questions about what we just did then?"

"Sure you can." Fergal had figured she'd have questions. He sat on one side of the bed, half-turned away from her so he wouldn't give way to temptation. Gus and Harley sat on her other side. "What do you need to know?"

"Well, what we just did, you giving me orders and making me call you all *Master* and stuff. What do you guys get out of it?" Gus and Harley choked back laughs. Fergal remained perfectly composed. "I mean, there's just one of me, but three of you. I've had four orgasms tonight…"

"It would have been five if I'd let you have your way," Fergal said, grinning.

"Oh yes, when you—your tongue. I didn't want you to stop, did I?" She giggled. "Anyway, you guys only got to have one each. Surely that's not enough to keep virile men like you content?"

"What we do is our form of BDSM. You know what that is?" She nodded. "We don't go to dungeons, but we would enjoy tying you up, clamping your nipples and other stuff like that, if you're willing. Being in control and having you do absolutely everything we ask of you is what we get off on. We might not get to have as many orgasms as you do, but let me tell you, the ones we do have are explosive because of our extreme form of foreplay."

"Being in the military and accustomed to taking and giving orders kinda got us into this," Harley explained.

"Right." Gus nodded. "You might feel like you're taking orders, but have you realized yet that you're actually the one in control?"

"Because I can call a halt any time I like by using the safe word?"

"Partly that," Fergal conceded. "But it's more that we have responsibility for your pleasure and safety. And that's a responsibility we take extremely seriously. Your pleasure is our pleasure, darlin'. It's the ultimate aphrodisiac."

"No commitment, no strings attached," she muttered.

"Something like that." Fergal leaned over and kissed her brow. "Now, get some sleep. You must be beat after all this activity. We'll let Max out and make sure the kittens are out of harm's way."

"Thank you," she replied, lifting a hand and touching each of them in turn. "For everything."

"Our pleasure," they said, heading for the door wearing nothing but their skin.

"Well," Harley said as they headed back to the great room. "I think I speak for us all when I say that was mind blowing."

"Amen." Gus slapped Harley's upraised hand.

"Say something, buddy," Harley said to Fergal as they retrieved their clothes. "You're awful quiet."

"I'm not sure this is such a good idea," he replied.

"With Briana, you mean?" Harley asked.

"She's a distraction."

"No way!" Harley and Gus said together.

"We ought to be concentrating on her problems, not on her."

"Come on, man," Harley said. "I know when you're trying to fool yourself, and that's what you're doing right now. She's gotten to you, slipped beneath your guard, and you're worried that you might actually feel something for her other than raging lust."

"That's a damned lie!"

"Is it?" Harley remained infuriatingly cool in the face of Fergal's rising temper. "Then why are you yelling at me?"

"Harley's got a point." Gus pulled his jeans over his naked body and opened the door to let Max out. "I thought you figured this Greg person was making problems for her so he could show himself up in a good light. We haven't lost sight of that, so what's the problem?" He paused in the open doorway. "Not scared of getting in too deep, are you?"

"You two are full of shit."

"And you're full of denial," Gus said quietly. "Cut yourself some slack, buddy, and admit to yourself that Briana's hot. Trust me, the world won't come to an end if you do."

"The relationship guru speaks," Fergal said with a cynical smile.

"You could do worse than listen," Harley replied. "Occasionally he talks sense."

Harley and Fergal sat in uneasy silence until Gus returned.

"Max has gone off somewhere, and it's fucking freezing out there," he explained.

"I did think it was just Greg trying to screw up Briana's plans at first," Fergal said, leaning his chin in his cupped hand as he articulated his thoughts. "But now I know someone tried to buy the lodge at an inflated price, it changes everything." He grabbed the paperwork from the real estate agent that Briana had left on the counter. "First thing tomorrow, Harley, get online and see if you can find out anything about the people who want to buy it."

"You got it."

Max scratched at the door. Gus got up to let him in, and the dog bounded up to the fire, shaking water off his coat and all over them.

"Ah, I thought it might rain." Fergal's head jerked backward. "Shit, we've left a lot of the new timber outside. Best get it under cover."

All three of them, dressed just in jeans and their boots, headed out into the pouring rain and heaved the timber into the storage shed. They were soaked through by the time they'd completed the task, but that didn't bother any of them. They'd suffered much worse during their days in the service.

"Hit the sack, guys," Fergal said, shedding his jeans again and leaving them to dry in front of the dwindling fire. "I need to report in to Raoul and ask him to send us a few odds and ends."

"What do you have in mind?" Harley asked, stripping down again also.

"Not sure yet, but you know me, I like to be prepared. Someone wants this lodge, and/or Briana. We need to find out who, which, and why so we can stop them. Harley, can you do a little creative hacking while you're at it?"

"Sure, what am I hacking into?"

"Greg's father has a marketing business in Glasgow. Find out as much as you can about it. Who his clients are, how much money he makes, you know the sort of thing."

"Consider it done."

* * * *

Briana's head buzzed, and her body continued to thrum with the afterglow of mind-blowing sex long after the guys had left her. They'd decided that she had to be tired without bothering to ask her if she actually was. She tried not to take offence at their arbitrary take. This being-told-what-to-do business would take some getting used to. She'd better make the adjustment pretty damned quick if she wanted to take full advantage, because she was unsure how much longer they'd stick around for.

She had so much to mull over, so much excitement to relive in her head. At last she understood what all the fuss was about when it came to sexual gymnastics. Better late than never, and she was anxious for as many repeat performances as they were willing to have her audition for. Being made to do as she was told, being punished if she didn't do it quickly enough—or even if she did—was a total turn-on.

Having not wanted the guys to invade her space, she now dreaded the day when it occurred to them that nothing was wrong here and it was time for them to move on. She was sure there was a ton more they could teach her before then, provided they weren't already bored with her, and she was the most enthusiastic student this side of the Mississippi.

"Stupid," she muttered. "There're busy guys with more exotic occupations awaiting them than the education of a sexually repressed female with freckles and wrinkly knees."

They were having some fun while they fulfilled their mission. She couldn't blame them for that, but unfortunately it wasn't so straightforward for Briana. She'd only been able to enter into the few sexual liaisons she'd previously experienced because she cared for her partners. So having let all three of them play with her, it could only mean that she had feelings for all three of them. Deep feelings of emotional oneness that defeated all understanding. How loopy was that?

Briana had never been in love with one man before, not really, and yet what she felt for these three was as close to complete love as she knew it. How was that possible? They were all so different and she knew little about their personal lives, and yet each one had imprinted her with an indelible mark she hoped would never fade. Her body was like a touch screen when she was around them, programed to explode in a blaze of glorious color when their capable hands so much as flicked across it.

"I'm a shameless hussy," she told the walls of the room, smiling as she did so. "And I'm loving every minute of it."

Briana didn't remember actually falling asleep, but at least she woke early. It was barely light outside, and she would make sure it was her who prepared breakfast for her guests this morning. Before she could throw the covers back, the door opened and Harley's muscled body filled the aperture.

"Ah, you're awake," he said, sending her a somnolent smile as he leaned down to kiss her lips, deep and slow. "Did you sleep well?"

When he broke the kiss, the smell of freshly-brewed coffee excited her taste buds.

"Yes, thanks. Oh, is that for me?" She took the mug from him with a nod of thanks. "Just what I need to kick-start the day. You're up early."

"No, it's gone nine," he replied, sitting on the bed beside her and running his fingers seductively down her arm.

"It can't be." He gaze flew to the window, even as goose bumps sprang up in the wake of his fingers. "It's still dark outside."

"It's pouring with rain."

Briana wanted to smack her head with the heel of her hand. For some reason her brain didn't appear to be functioning, and she'd failed to recognize the sound of rain pounding against the windowpane.

"No roofing today then."

"I guess not."

Damn, his fingers had reached the side of her breast and were teasing it with a featherlight touch. Two days ago, any delays with the roofing would have had her screaming with frustration. Now she was glad. They must realize that no one was trying to sabotage her efforts here, so helping with the roof gave them a legitimate reason to hang around for a bit longer.

If they wanted to.

"I ought to get up," she said without much conviction in her tone.

"No rush." His hand was now cupping one breast. Briana closed her eyes and felt the reaction all the way to her toes.

"Where's Max? He usually sleeps with me."

"I think he spent the night in Gus's room."

She grinned. "Not very faithful, is he?"

"He's not stupid, either. Gus is the one who spends all his time in the kitchen."

She smiled. "Yes, there is that, I suppose."

His gaze burned into her profile, dark and intense. "We are," he said softly.

Her breath caught in her throat and her gaze locked with his. "Are what?"

"Faithful."

What does that mean? Impulsively Briana threw the covers back. "Join me," she said. "If I'm not allowed to get up then you have to keep me company."

"Hey, taking matters into your own hands will get you spanked."

She giggled. "A girl can but hope."

"You sure you're not too sore?" he asked, already shedding his clothes.

"For that?" she asked, pointing to his massive erection and licking her lips. "I think I can probably manage."

"Hmm, you'll get me in trouble with the boss. I was told to bring you your coffee, nothing more."

"Do you always do as you're told?"

He flashed a rueful grin. "Apparently not."

The bed dipped as he maneuvered his large body right up close to hers, turned her on her side and wrapped his arms around her waist from behind. His thick cock pressed against her ass, and Briana couldn't help pushing back against it. He tapped her butt, and she instantly stilled.

"I want to touch you all over," he said. "Did you know that touching decreases stress and releases feel good hormones like oxytocin, which is nature's bonding agent? It increases sexual responsiveness and sensitivity."

"I feel pretty responsive and sensitive already," she said, squirming against his hands as they covered her breasts and tweaked hard at the nipples.

"Can't be too careful." He rolled her onto her back and pulled the covers aside. "Spread your legs and bend your knees up for me, sweet thing."

He jumped off the bed again, pulled the belt from the loops in his jeans, and returned to her almost immediately.

"Arms above your head." Briana knew what he intended to do and gladly complied. He looped the belt around both of her wrists and then attached it to the headboard. "Now you're at my complete mercy. Comfortable?"

"Yes, Master Harley." He must be able to see all her freckles quite clearly now, but, astonishingly, he didn't seem to mind them.

"I've got something else here that you might enjoy." He reached into the pocket of his jeans and extracted two clothespins.

"Tell me again that you only came to deliver my coffee."

"I was a boy scout. I like to be prepared."

"Prepared for what?" But she knew.

"I'm gonna attach these to your nipples, darlin'. Tell me how they make you feel."

Briana braced herself for pain but none was forthcoming. Presumably she looked as surprised as she felt because Harley explained why that was.

"They cut off the blood flow to your nipples and make them more sensitive." He ran his tongue across one of them, and the sensation was so intense that she almost elevated from the bed. "I guess actions speak louder than words," he said, chuckling.

Harley abandoned her tits, knelt at her feet and kissed, licked, and sucked each toe in turn. Briana closed her eyes and tried to slow her respiration. She'd already learned that the slower she breathed, the more she relaxed and the greater the sensation. When he started to kiss his way up her calves, pausing at the back of her ugly knees for a little suction and tongue-twirling, her overstimulated heart felt in danger of exploding. His tongue worked its way up her inner thighs, lapping up the juices spilling freely from her pussy.

"Your skin is so damned soft," he said, lifting his head and licking her honey from his lips. "I can smell your musk and taste the essence of you. You're making me so fucking hard, darlin'. I don't know whether to punish you for being such a tease or fuck your brains out."

"You could do both."

"Silence!"

"Sorry, Master Harley."

He returned to her inner thighs, gliding his tongue teasingly closer to her cunt. Briana rolled her head from side to side and moaned. It was beyond her to remain passively silent in the face of such provocation. She would defy any woman to manage it. She sensed his nose hovering over her pussy, inhaling her scent. She gasped when his tongue flicked across her clit, gently at first. When the strokes became firmer, Briana could feel the texture of his tongue as it swirled and sucked at her most sensitive place. He circled it around her swollen nub like a hunter stalking its prey, a seductive, teasing dance that she wasn't permitted to participate in. When he wrapped his lips around the base of her clit and sucked, sensation streaked through her in dizzying waves.

"Ah!" She lifted her hips and thrust her pussy into his mouth. "I can't take much more, Master Harley. I know I shouldn't speak, but you need to know that you're driving me over the edge."

She regretted speaking when the torture immediately stopped. He tipped her onto her side again and spanked her ass. Hard. Her pegged nipples zinged with displaced reaction.

"Do you have something to say to me, Briana?"

"Sorry, Master. Please punish me for disobeying the rules."

He spanked her harder still. It was glorious torture, but nothing compared to her reaction when she felt his thick cock slide between her legs. Was life allowed to be this good? Briana had a terrible premonition that she'd be made to pay for her few days of madness.

* * * *

Harley grabbed a condom from the pocket of his jeans, tore the packet open with his teeth, and rolled it down his length. Rejoining Briana on the bed, he lifted her upper leg, giving himself space to slide the head of his cock into her tight cunt. He couldn't remember the last time he'd been so hard, so totally focused on a particular woman. He'd barely slept for thinking about her. Even so, he hadn't intended for this to happen when he'd brought coffee to her this morning. *Yeah, right!* What else could he realistically have imagined? Briana was sex on stilts and he didn't think he'd ever be able to get enough of her.

With one fluid glide he slid all the way into her, and it felt like coming home. He tweaked one of her pegged nipples, eliciting an anguished cry from his lovely captive. He didn't need to ask if he'd hurt her. She'd already learned to transmute the pain to pleasure and was hot, wet, and *so* ready for him. He worked his way deeper, enjoying the way her silken fist closed greedily around his thick heat, a willing hostage to her femininity. They moved together until she'd absorbed his entire length, which is when he realized he was in trouble. Harley prided himself on his staying power, but the moment he'd sunk all the way home a disturbing thrill rocked him sideways and he knew his control was in danger of slipping.

What the fuck was she doing to him?

He pulled her hair aside, wound it around one hand, and deposited hot kisses down the length of her neck. His balls were tight and heavy, he was so damned close, and so was she. He could tell when her muscles tightened around him and she emitted a string of needy little moans. He tugged on her hair and worked deeper into her with strong upwards thrusts.

"Stay with me, honey. Let's do this together."

"Yes, Master. I want to give you pleasure."

"You do, just by being you."

Harley sucked her earlobe and slammed into her as hard as he could. She cried out and he felt her body convulse.

"Oh God, Harley, that's astonishing. I can't stop coming."

Perspiration slicked her body as she continued to ride the crest of her orgasm. Unable to hold back, he let himself go, and with a guttural moan he shot his load into the condom.

"Oh, darlin'," he said, breathing hard.

Harley took a moment to recover, then got up and disposed of the condom. He returned with a cloth to clean her up, released her hands, and removed the clothespins.

"Your nipples will be real sensitive when the blood flows back into them," he warned.

"Yeah, but that's not a bad thing," she replied, touching one and smiling, presumably because she was enjoying the experience.

"I like to see you touch yourself like that."

"Then I'm glad to have pleased you."

"Oh, you please me, darlin'. Never doubt it for a moment."

"Thank you," she said, looking almost shy now it was over.

"You're entirely welcome." He lay back down and circled her shoulders with his arm. She rested her head on his chest and drew patterns on it with her forefinger, tugging at the wiry hairs that adorned his torso.

"I know nothing at all about you," she said. "Where are you from?"

"My family live in Philadelphia. I was raised there."

"And, don't tell me, you were the quarterback for the high school football team."

"Nope, actually I sucked at sports, mainly because I didn't get to play any."

"Why ever not? I should have thought you'd be a natural. You're certainly built to butt heads."

"You didn't see me when I was a kid." Harley shrugged. "I was what you'd call a late developer. I was scrawny and didn't sprout vertically until way after the other kids. My family is made up of academics, and that's what they wanted me to be."

"You can't just *be* an academic. You have to have the necessary brain power."

"Well, with all due modesty, my IQ is pretty impressive."

"Show off!" She circled one of his nipples and leaned in to nip at it playfully, causing his cock to twitch.

"You did ask."

"So, what happened? How did you finish up in the marines?"

"I had no particular interest in academia. Seemed dull and dry to me. I wanted to have fun, like the other kids, but I guess I was too much of an oddball. All the others either picked on me, or ignored me."

"Kids can be real mean like that."

"Yeah, well, that all changed when a certain Fergal Stanton moved to town with his family. Now he *was* the school quarterback."

She rolled her eyes. "Of course he was."

"Handsome, popular, girls hanging off every orifice. I'm sure you get the picture."

"And he helped you out?"

"Yeah, we got partnered on a school science project. All the other kids felt sorry for him getting landed with the geek, but Fergal seemed to genuinely like me and didn't give a fuck what anyone else thought about his choice of buddies. You can have no idea how much I admired his attitude. And, of course, the more he did as he pleased, the more people clung to him."

"And you were getting the respect you deserved."

"Yeah, Fergal and I spent a whole semester working on that project, getting to know and like one another. I suspected his motives at first, because no one chose to be friendly with me." Harley laughed. "Course, it helped that I knew more about empirical data than he did. I assumed he'd drop me once the project was over, but that didn't happen."

Briana laughed. "I don't think Fergal is that shallow."

"I know that now, but back then...Anyway, I told him how much I hated being puny. He suggested I go along to the gym with him, which is something I'd never have done alone for fear of being laughed at."

"But with Fergal as your mentor, you were safe."

"Right, and I started to develop muscles at the same time as my height finally increased. I went off to college shortly after that but fell out with my family when I chose not to apply for jobs in the science sector."

"What was Fergal doing at the time?"

"He'd gone to a different college. We met up again back home in Richmond, and Fergal told me he'd already decided to enlist."

"What made him do that?"

"Aw, honey, if you want to know, you need to ask him."

"I will. I want to know all about all of you."

"Well, you pretty well know all there is about me now. I went against my family's wishes and enlisted alongside Fergal. And the rest, as they say, is history."

"Are your family still mad at you?"

Harley shrugged. "They're wrapped up in their own little worlds. My parents, brother, and sister are all scientists. I broke the mold and they lost interest in me. They seem to think I've wasted my talents." He sent her a puerile grin. "I disagree. We meet up occasionally. I think Mom's glad I'm no longer a serving marine, but apart from that we don't have a lot of interaction."

"That's sad."

"No, honey, it's the way it is. We can choose our friends, but we're stuck with the families we're given."

"I get the impression that Fergal and Gus are more of a family to you now."

"Too right. We make a good team. Gus does the catering, I'm the geek, and Fergal's in charge. He also happens to be an ace with anything that has an engine in it."

"So you enjoy working and playing together."

"We've been in a lot of dangerous situations together, and had one another's backs, so yeah, I guess you could say that we know one another pretty well."

"Do you always share your women?"

"Aw, now that's a leading question, honey."

"But a reasonable one."

"Not always, but we are drawn to the same type of woman, so it happens a fair bit."

Damn, Harley wished the words back. Her expression closed down, and he knew she wouldn't thank him for implying that she was just another conquest. Far as he was concerned she wasn't. She's stirred something deep inside him, and he wanted to hang around and get to know her way better. But that wasn't a decision he could make alone. He had a duty to his partners and had no idea how they felt.

"Come on, lazybones," he said, pushing back the covers. "Gus has cooked breakfast for us all, and you know how he is about his food."

Briana laughed and also got up. "I'll take a quick shower and be right there," she said.

Chapter Twelve

"Sorry," Harley said, grinning as he reentered the great room. "I got unavoidably detained."

Fergal looked up from the wall he'd taken over plastering for Briana and quirked a brow. "Can't imagine what kept you."

"I can," Gus growled from the kitchen. "Ain't fair."

"Someone reliable had to reassure the lady," Harley said, smirking.

"Fuck you!" Gus replied.

"I'll pass, thanks."

Fergal put his plastering tray down and joined Gus and Harley at the kitchen counter. "I need you to run into town after breakfast," he said to Gus.

"Sure. What do you need me to do?"

"There'll be a package for us at the UPS store sent overnight by Raoul."

"Okay, I'll pick that up and go to the grocery store. What else?"

"I need you to pay a visit to the barber shop."

"Aw, I like my hair long."

"Greg thinks there are only two of us out here. No one knows about you."

"Yeah, I guess he's pretty easy to overlook," Harley said, grinning.

Gus shot him the finger. "Just because you got your end away, it don't mean—"

"Gentleman," Fergal said impatiently. "I need you all to be clear on this before Briana joins us. She's not ready to hear about my worries regarding this place."

"You think someone's definitely out to get her?" Harley asked, sobering.

"Yeah, and I don't think they're gonna sit back and wait for us to knock the place into shape before they make their move."

"Is that what we're planning to do?" Gus asked. "I figured you'd be keen to get the hell out of Dodge, before you get too attached to our favorite inhabitant."

"Go to the barber shop, Gus," Fergal replied. "Seek out Briana's granny's friends, Seth and Maurice. If there's anything going on, I'll bet my bank balance they'll have a theory about it. Buy them as many coffees as it takes and let them ramble on. They obviously care about Briana, otherwise they wouldn't have alerted her old man to her problems."

"I'm on it."

"On what?"

They all turned at the sound of Briana's voice. Fergal had to quell the lustful thoughts inspired just by looking at her, all sleepy and gloriously rumpled, her lips still swollen from Harley's kisses. He'd ignored Gus's earlier jibe about the need to leave, mainly because he didn't want to go anywhere but wasn't ready to admit it. Damn it, she'd gotten to him, and he needed to be sure she was safe. Was he inventing dangers where none existed? He didn't think so, but his judgment was impaired simply because Briana was perilously close to unlocking something inside him that he wasn't sure ought to be released.

His frozen heart had been thawed by a redheaded siren with piercing green eyes, glorious freckles, and self-esteem issues. He ought to be terrified. He wasn't. Fergal didn't do commitment anymore, and yet the idea of a permanent relationship with Briana filled him with urgent longing. Not all women were as duplicitous as his former wife. Briana definitely wasn't. He'd wised up over the past five years and had become a damned good judge of character.

Only problem was, he, Harley, and Gus were a team. If the three of them wanted Briana as a permanent presence in their lives, Fergal didn't think that would be such a bad thing. Three of them ought to be able to keep her happy, surely? But what if they didn't? *Forget it, Stanton. It's not in the script for you to settle down and be happy, like an average family man.*

"Hey, babe," Fergal said, moving in for a casual kiss. "How you feeling this morning?"

"Wonderful." She stood on her toes to return his kiss, then turned to Gus and did the same thing with him. "Can't remember the last time I slept so well."

"No strained muscles or soreness?" Gus asked.

"Nope." She bent to tickle Max's ears and then scooped up one of the kittens before it dived headlong into the plaster tray. "Say, you don't need to do the plastering. That's something I can manage."

Fergal sent her a smile designed to imply it was no big deal. "Have to do something to pass the time until the weather clears. The forecast is for rain all day. It won't move through until late tonight."

"I can think of a way to pass the time," Gus said, grinning.

"Get your mind out the gutter, buddy," Fergal replied.

Gus winked at Briana. "I like playing in the gutter and hanging out with you guys there."

"Something smells good," Briana said.

"Breakfast is served, ma'am." Gus offered her a flourishing bow and ushered her to a seat at the counter.

Fergal washed his hands, and they all tucked in to Gus's fluffy scrambled eggs, bacon, and fried potatoes.

"Wow." Briana leaned back and patted her belly. "If you keep feeding me like this I'll get even fatter."

Fergal glowered at her. "Briana, what are you?" he asked.

She immediately lowered her eyes, blushing furiously. "Desirable, Master," she said, addressing to the comment to her folded hands.

"Yes, you are. Now say it again like you mean it."

"You're asking too much of me, Sir. I know it isn't true, so how can I mean it?"

"You think what we did to you last night, what Harley did to you this morning, is just a game for us?"

"Yes." She shook her head. "No. Hell, I don't know. You're confusing me."

Fergal sighed. "If you weren't full of breakfast, I'd put you over my knee right now and spank some sense into you."

"We could make her strip and stand in the corner," Harley suggested.

"We could certainly do that." Fergal rubbed his jaw, thinking about it. "In fact…Hello, we've got company."

Fergal went to the window just in time to see a sheriff's car pull up outside. "Get out of sight, Gus," he said urgently. "Remember, babe. There are just the two of us here with you. I don't want anyone to know about Gus."

"Oh, all right. But it's only the sheriff."

"Does he make a habit of calling on you?"

"Well, no but—"

Harley whisked the breakfast plates into the sink. Fergal knew she'd have to invite the sheriff in, and he just might be astute enough to notice four place settings.

"Good thinking," he said to Harley.

Harley grinned, still obviously on a high after his inventive method of waking Briana up. "I'm the brains of this operation, remember."

Fergal rolled his eyes. "Like I could forget."

Briana opened the door before the sheriff could knock. "Hey, Sheriff," she said. "What brings you all the way out here in such foul weather?"

"Mind if I come in for a moment, Briana?"

"Of course not."

She opened the door wider, and a large man with a gut that hung over his belt stepped into the room, the radio on his vest spitting static. He removed his hat to reveal a baldpate and shook rain from his headgear.

"Is that fresh coffee I smell? Ah, you have company, I see," he said, eyeing Fergal and Harley with open interest.

Like you didn't know.

"The name's Stanton," Fergal said, not offering the lawman his hand. "Something we can do for you?"

"You staying here for long?"

"Any reason why that's any of your concern?"

"I just like to know who's hanging out in my patch, is all. Goes with the job."

Right, and who told you we were here? "Well, we haven't decided yet, Sheriff, but when we do, you'll be the first to know."

Briana laced a mug of coffee with cream and two sugars and handed it to the sheriff.

"Thanks, honey." He glanced around the room. "Quite a job you've set yourself here."

"Yes, it's long overdue but will be worth it."

"Just a friendly word of advice," the sheriff said when they'd exhausted the subject of the weather and Fergal had made it plain they weren't going to leave him alone with Briana. "I hear tell that you wanted to hire in labor and pay cash in hand." He shook his head, causing his jowls to wobble. "Wouldn't recommend it if you're trying to turn the lodge into a commercial venture. The IRS has long arms and longer memories."

"I'm curious. Under what circumstances would you recommend it, Sheriff?" Harley asked.

"Officially, none. Unofficially, if someone just wants a bit of work done on their own home, well…it's a different story."

"So that wouldn't be against the law, but Briana hiring on an ad-hoc basis would?"

"That's not what I said, young fella. In fact, I didn't catch your name."

Harley folded his arms across his chest. "I didn't give it."

"I hope you ain't paying these dudes to help you out, Briana."

"No, I'm not doing that." She smiled at the sheriff. "It would be against the law."

The sheriff clearly knew when he'd met his match. He downed his coffee, picked up his hat, and stood up. "Well, I'd best be getting along. Criminals to catch, paperwork to keep on top of." He stood with his hand on the door, glaring at Harley and Fergal in a futile attempt to intimidate them. Fergal assumed he'd run the plate on their truck to try and find out more about them. Good luck with that. It would just lead him back to their skiing business in Columbia Falls. "Thanks for the coffee, Briana, and just remember what I said."

"What was that all about?" Gus asked, emerging from the bedroom corridor.

"A fishing expedition," Harley replied. "Someone told him we were here and to find out what we wanted and how long we planned to stay."

Fergal nodded. "I agree. Who in Fort Peck has that sort of influence over the sheriff, darlin'?"

Briana looked blank. "I have absolutely no idea. Pearson's been sheriff here for years. He's harmless enough. Used to come out here a lot and chat with Gran. I've never heard anything about him being corrupt."

"If it was common knowledge that he took backhanders or reelection funds from anyone, something would have to be done about it," Fergal replied. "Best get off to town, Gus, and deal with those errands I set you."

"I'm on my way," he replied, picking up the keys to their truck and heading for the door. "Play nice without me, children."

* * * *

"I'll help you with the plastering," Briana told Fergal.

"Okay, darlin'. Harley's got some online stuff to do, so you and I can handle the manual stuff."

They worked side by side, while Harley occupied the kitchen counter with his laptop, his fingers flying across the keys as he muttered to himself and jotted down notes.

"Harley was telling me about his childhood and how you helped him out," Briana said to Fergal as they worked side by side. "What about your family? Are they still in Philly?"

"My dad passed a couple of years back, and Mom remarried." Fergal curled his lip. "She remarried so fast that it made me wonder...Well, anyway, she's in Florida with her new husband. I don't see much of her."

"Do you have siblings?"

"Nope. It's just me and, from what I've seen of other family relationships," he said, nodding toward Harley but probably thinking about Gus and his sister, "I don't think I missed out."

"Oh, I don't know. I always wished there was someone else around, close to my age."

"Because you didn't have parents," Fergal said, his dark eyes softening as they regarded her. "Of course you'd feel that way."

They worked on in companionable silence for some time. Max wandered in and out to check on progress, looking hopefully toward the kitchen, presumably in the expectation of finding Gus there. The kittens had been locked in a bedroom to keep them away from the wet plaster, and the only sound in the room was the scraping of pallet knives and Harley's fingers on his keyboard. Occasionally he cursed, and once or twice he let out a triumphant *ah-hah.* Fergal ignored him, presumably because he knew he'd report his findings when he was good and ready.

Briana burned to know what he was looking for, but Fergal hadn't seen fit to enlighten her, which was infuriating. He might think he could turn her into an obedient sex slave in the bedroom—hell, there was no *think* about it—but when it came to her livelihood, it was a different matter. She *would* speak her mind and express her opinions, no question about it.

Fergal's cell phone rang. He put down his plaster tray and moved aside to answer it.

"Hey, Raoul," she heard him say. "What you got for me? Yeah, Gus has just gone to pick it up." He listened. "Not yet, Harley's on it now. I'll let you know if I need anything else."

He cut the connection, but before Briana could ask what that was all about, they heard the truck pull up outside. Gus ran in, looking bedraggled, a heap of grocery store bags and a UPS parcel bundled in his hands.

"I have information," he said.

Harley looked up from his keyboard. "So do I."

Chapter Thirteen

"It's lunchtime," Fergal said. "Babe, if you knock some sandwiches together, we need to take care of a few jobs outside. Then we'll talk."

Briana frowned. "What's so urgent outside in this weather?"

"Won't be long." Fergal ripped open the UPS parcel and the array of gizmos and electronic devises he'd asked Raoul to supply spilled from it. Under the protection of the overhang porch, the three of them set up a near-invisible wireless camera focused on the door to the lodge. Then they set up another in the store where they'd placed the roof timbers.

"Okay," Fergal said. "Let's get back inside, and Harley can do whatever he has to do to make sure the feed comes through to his laptop."

"It works just fine," Harley said a short time later.

Briana slapped a platter of sandwiches on the counter, clearly pissed with them for not telling her what was going on. The guys made the odd observation as they consumed their lunch, but Briana said nothing at all.

When they were finished, she stacked the dishwasher while Harley brought in logs and got the fire going.

"Now we can talk," Fergal said, pulling her down on the settee beside him. The fire was already blazing up the chimney, warding off the damp and chill brought on by the rain that still pounded down. "You go first, Gus. What did you discover in Fort Peck?"

"Plenty. Seth and Maurice say *hi,* by the way," he told Briana.

"You went to speak with those two?" She dealt him a quizzical look. "Why, for goodness sake?"

"They told your dad you needed help," Fergal said, placing a hand on her thigh and leaving it there because…well, because it felt like a natural thing to do. "I figured there had to be a reason for that."

"Yes, they're interfering old duffers with more time on their hands than they know what to do with." Briana rolled her eyes. "And men accuse women of being gossips."

"They're not quite so into their dotage as you think, hon," Gus replied. "They see everything that goes on and know when something's not right."

She inhaled sharply. "What do you mean?"

"They spoke with your grandmother before she passed. That guy who wanted to buy this place wasn't what he appeared to be, according to Seth and Maurice."

"How would they know?"

"They saw him in town several times."

"Yes, with the real estate agent." The kittens had been released from the bedroom, and one of them jumped onto Briana's lap. She absently stroked his ears. "If he wanted to buy a property, he would be."

"No, darlin'. He wasn't seen with the real estate guy." Gus paused to extract the other kitten from the log basket. "He was with Greg Stone's old man."

Fergal jerked upright. "There's a connection between the two?"

Gus shrugged. "Apparently."

"Did Seth and Maurice get his name?" Fergal asked.

"Well, they weren't exactly introduced, but when they found out he was sniffing around this place they asked Briana's gran. Seems his name's Seagrove and—"

"And he's one of Stone's clients," Harley finished for him. "I found him in their client base but haven't gotten around to checking him out yet."

"Make it your next job," Fergal said. "There has to be a connection."

"How did you get sight of Mr. Stone's client base?" Briana asked Harley.

He sent her a lazy smile. "I told you, hon. I'm a genius."

"And modest, too." Briana shook her head. "Computer hacking was illegal, last time I checked."

Harley winked at her. "Only if you get caught."

Fergal could tell she was trying hard to disapprove but convinced no one, including herself, most likely. "The end justifies the means, darlin'," he said. "We now know there's a connection between the guy who's so concerned about you that he can't leave you alone for five minutes and the one who wants to buy this place." Fergal paused. "You'd think he might have mentioned it."

"Yes, it does seem odd," she conceded. "But still—"

"Anything else to tell us, Gus?" Fergal asked.

"I showed the guys the picture Harley took on his phone of Greg and mystery man. They thought he looked familiar but couldn't see enough of his face to be sure."

"Fuck," Fergal said quietly.

"Ah, but fear not. I actually saw the guy getting into a beaten up truck as I drove out of town. At least I'm pretty sure it was him."

Fergal slapped his shoulder. "Tell me you caught sight of the tag."

Gus pulled a disgruntled expression. "What do you take me for, an amateur?" He pulled a notebook from his pocket and reeled off the number.

"I'm on it," Harley said, hitting his computer keyboard at speed.

"We don't know that he has anything to do with Greg's dad," Briana pointed out. "Or that Greg's dad has anything to do with wanting this place."

"We don't actually *know* the president's a democrat," Gus replied, "but the evidence is fairly compelling. Besides, this isn't a court of law, and my gut tells me we're onto something."

"The truck's registered to a Kyle Bruce," Harley said an impressively short time later. "An address is Winter Vale."

"It's a trailer park just outside of town," Briana said.

"The guy's got a rap sheet. Served two years for petty larceny."

"Has he indeed." Fergal flexed his jaw. "Now why would a fine upstanding member of the local community be deep in conversation with an ex-con?"

"Not quite so upstanding," Harley replied. "I ran that check on Stone's company earlier. They're deeply in the mire, financially speaking. They lost a couple of big accounts recently, which left them stretched. Stone senior's home is now mortgaged up to the hilt, they've exceeded their business overdraft, and the bank's getting antsy."

Briana looked bewildered. "What's going on? I thought Greg's dad was wealthy."

"That's probably what he wants people to think," Gus replied. "Appearances are everything to people who like to think they're a big fish in a small pond. Still an' all, a lot of businesses took a pounding when the economy tanked. Seems his is one of them."

"Surprised the bank extended more credit," Harley remarked.

"I have a feeling that Stone senior has a lot of local people in his back pocket, including the sheriff," Fergal remarked.

Briana's eyes widened. "You think he's responsible for the sheriff visit today?"

"I'm not sure what to think, but I know where to start looking." Fergal removed his hand from Briana's thigh, where his fingers had spent the last quarter of an hour drawing intricate patterns all over it. "Shall we go and pay Kyle Bruce a friendly visit in his trailer, see what he has to say for himself, Harley?"

"You want to let him know you're on to him?" Gus asked. "Is that wise?"

No, Fergal didn't think it was wise, but he had a bad feeling about this. Short of patrolling the outside of the property twenty-four-seven, there was no way they could guarantee Briana's safety. The cameras only covered a very small part of a large property. These people were obviously desperate to get their hands on the place—hence Greg's almost constant attention toward Briana. Fergal felt a violent rage surge through him when he thought of that jerk getting anywhere near her, and it simply wasn't a risk he was prepared to take.

Their time limitations would explain the sheriff's fishing trip this morning. If Fergal had said they were about to leave, Stone could have afforded to bide his time until they had just one little lady to frighten. Even so, Briana was no pushover and persuading her to part with the property she loved would require more than a verbal charm campaign. People like Stone didn't believe in damaging their manicures and got the Kyle Bruces of this world to do their dirty work for them. Ergo, it was simply a case of Fergal *persuading* Bruce to give up everything he knew about his assignment to scare Briana. Fergal needed to know why they wanted the place so badly.

"Yeah, I think it's wise," Fergal said in a glacial tone.

"Take Gus. I need to run checks on this Seagrove guy."

"Call Raoul and have him and Zeke run the check. Gus already got soaking wet once today."

"Take care," Briana said anxiously. "I still think you're overreacting, but if there is something going on I don't want you getting hurt because of me."

"Aw, honey," Harley said, kissing the back of her neck and wrapping his arms around her from behind. "That's so sweet, but don't you go worrying about us. We're big boys and can take care of ourselves."

"Keep a close watch on the cameras, Gus," Fergal warned, reaching for his jacket.

* * * *

"What cameras?" Briana asked, returning to the fire with Gus after they'd waved Fergal and Harley off.

"Just a few little spying devices we put up outside to help intercept intruders."

"Now you're frightening me."

Gus sat down and pulled her with him, wrapping a protective arm around her shoulders. "Frightened is good. Frightened people stay alert."

"You don't seem too alert," she remarked, when his free hand slid beneath her top and his fingers inched their way toward her breasts.

"Hey, I take my duties seriously. Have to make sure you don't have any concealed weapons."

She laughed, anticipation coursing through her as Gus's questing fingers continued to roam. "I'm not the enemy."

"That's what you say, but I'm a cautious guy." He waggled his brows at her. "You have no idea what sorts of stunts a desperate enemy is capable of pulling."

"You think my breasts are the enemy."

"A very good question." He drilled her with a sexy smile as he pulled her top over her head and threw it on the floor. "Best make sure."

"See, I don't have any hidden goodies."

"I wouldn't say that," he replied, closing his fingers over one of her tits and tweaking the nipple. "These babies could pulverize any man who doesn't keep his wits about him. Hell of a way to go."

Gus didn't remove her bra. Instead he pulled her tits out of the cups. The nipples protruded over the top, dark pink, rock solid, exquisitely painful. Briana moaned when he attached his lips to one of them and bit down. She sank her fingers into his hair and pushed his head closer. Gus made a grunting sound, removed his arm from around her shoulders, and leaned into the corner of the couch. He pulled her with him so she was almost lying on top of him. Still feasting on her tits, one hand ran over her ass and squeezed her buttocks, pushing her against his arousal.

Briana didn't know herself. Only a few hours ago, Harley had rocked her world. Now Gus was doing the same thing, and she was more than ready to meet him halfway. She fumbled between them, reaching for his zipper. Taking matters into her own hands was probably a punishable offence, but she was too turned on to care. Before she could get very far, he raised his head and shook it from side to side.

"Can't wait, huh? Wasn't Harley enough for you this morning?"

"I want you, too," she said, surprising herself with the brazen admission.

"Yeah, I got that part. Stand up, darlin', in front of the fire where I can see you." She did so, remembering at the last minute to lower her eyes. "Hmm, now don't you make the prettiest picture. Take your hair down." Briana pulled out the clip, and her crowning glory cascaded all over the place in a riot of corkscrew curls. "That's good. Now lose the bra for me and play with your tits."

The new, improved Briana did so without a twinge of embarrassment. She didn't even care about her freckles, or her knees. Never removing her gaze from his languorous one she reached back to unfasten her bra, turned her back to him, and threw it over her shoulder, aiming for his lap. Then she turned slowly back again, her breasts squeezed between her hands until the nipples almost touch one another. Gus sucked in a sharp breath and then let out a low whistle that bolstered her courage.

"Play with the nipples. Pinch them as hard as you can take it." She did as he asked, moistening her lips with the tip of her tongue as she reveled in his obvious excitement. "Yeah, darlin', that's so damned sexy. You enjoy exhibiting yourself, babe?"

"If it makes you happy, Master Gus."

"It sure does, darlin'." He unzipped, proving that he'd gone commando when a huge erection sprang free from the opening. He fisted it, giving her a good view of what she hoped would soon be forcing its way deep into her pussy.

"You wet?" he asked.

Briana lowered her eyes again. "Yes, Master. Is that a bad thing?"

"Why are you wet, Briana?"

"Because I want you to fuck me, Master Gus."

"Didn't your gran tell you that little girls who want don't get?" Gus waved a finger at her. "Unfasten your jeans, pull them down to expose your ass, and then come over here."

It was awkward, walking with her jeans hanging around her hips, but Briana was too excited to care. As soon as she reached Gus's position, he wrapped an arm around her waist and pulled her over his knee. She squirmed when his large hand slid beneath her panties and a finger played with the spongy area between her ass and pussy. It felt wonderful but stopped almost before it had started, causing a small groan of protest to slip past her guard. He pulled her panties down to join her jeans and something came down hard over her bare ass. Not his hand, but something thinner and sharper.

"Did a little shopping while I was out today," he said. "This is a whip used on horses. You like?"

Briana nodded, closing her eyes as pleasure fizzed through her bloodstream, wiping away the initial discomfort. "I love, Master Gus."

He chuckled. "Had a feeling you might." He whipped her again. "Roll with the pain, darlin', and think about my cock fucking you, like it will be real soon." Another whip. "Your ass sure does look pretty with pink stripes across it."

She heard the whip clatter to the floor and felt his lips sucking and teeth gently biting her sore buttocks. Before she had a chance to get used to the feeling, something cool trickled over her ass. He rubbed it into the crack and circled her anus with a slick finger. She instinctively tensed up, unsure if she wanted to go this far.

"Relax, babe, and let me in."

She tried really hard to do so, sighing when he forced his finger past her tightly-coiled muscle and explored inside.

"If you really want to play with the three of us, then you're gonna have to let us fuck your sweet ass," he said. "You think you can do that?"

She had absolutely no idea, but she'd give it a try. Anything they wanted from her, she would give it, even if there was no pleasure in it for her. Except everything they'd done so far had blown her mind. She suspected that this would be no different, provided she could get past her reservations about it. As though reading her thoughts, she felt Gus insert something other than his finger. Again she tensed against it.

"Trust me, darlin'," he said, his voice earthy with vibrancy. "You'll be glad you did."

She wanted to trust him, but it was hard. Then a finger toyed with her throbbing clit, distracting her. Whatever he was using on her ass slid deeper, and suddenly it didn't hurt anymore. A startled *oh* slipped past her lips.

"Exactly." His voice was full of smug satisfaction as he righted her on his lap and pulled her jeans and panties off. "Go sit in the other corner and make yourself come for me," he said. "Use this."

He tossed a vibrator her way. Briana hesitated. Masturbation was a deeply personal thing, wasn't it? She'd grown pretty adept at it over the years but wasn't sure she needed an audience.

"Do it, Briana," he said sternly. "Don't make me ask again."

"What about…" She didn't know what to call it and her words stalled.

"It's a butt plug, darlin'. It'll distend you for later on." *Later on. What are they planning?* "It stays right where it is. Doesn't it feel good?"

Briana nodded. "Actually, yes, it does."

"It's filled with oil. Your body will heat it up, and you get the benefit of all those hot vibes."

"Hot vibes I can take," she said, scrambling into position and sliding the vibrator into her cunt, turning it to the slowest speed.

"Tell me what you usually do when you bring yourself off. Do you use a vibrator or your fingers?"

"Both, Master Gus." She slid two fingers between her pussy lips, rubbing them against her distended clit and sighing when sparks fluttered deep in her gut. "I like to rub my clit with my own juices and put the vibrator on low, just like I am now." With her knees bent and legs spread wide, Brianna watched his reaction as he got an up close view of what she was doing. "I like to feel the vibrator stretching me and my fingers upping the heat." Her hand worked a little faster. So did Gus's breathing. His gaze was glued to her pussy, like he'd never seen one before. She felt empowered by the admiration in his eye.

"Once I get into a decent rhythm I like to pinch my nipples," she said, lifting a hand to do so. Her fingers moved faster, and she turned the vibrator up a notch. She lifted her hips to drive it deeper, panting as heat spread through her, providing a deeply disturbing jolt as her orgasm began to unfurl.

"You like me watching you?" Gus asked in a thick voice, massaging his throbbing cock. Briana could see the thick vein that ran its length standing proud. His cock pulsated, and there was a drop of pre-cum sparkling on its head.

"Yes, Master Gus," she replied, panting as pleasure threatened to explode and there was nothing she could do to stop it steamrolling through her body.

"Did I mention you're not allowed to come until I give you permission?"

Briana's desperation made her forget the rules. "That's so not fair!"

"Slow down, honey. You're in too much of a hurry. It'll be better if you take it slow."

"I can't. That thing in my backside is making me wild. Sorry, Master, you'll have to punish me later, but I just can't...argh!"

She closed her eyes and threw her head back as her pussy clenched and her orgasm exploded. She pushed the vibrator as deep as it would go, feeling overloaded with the plug in her backside competing for the limited space.

"Naughty girl," Gus said, waving a finger at her and grinning when she opened her eyes again.

"Sorry, Sir."

"Get over here and straddle me."

Briana removed the vibrator, and slid into position, her cunt hovering over his massive penis, now covered in a thin layer of latex. She gripped the back of the couch and held her weight on her knees, still feeling the aftershock of her self-induced orgasm rippling through her. Already anticipating the feel of Gus's glorious cock filling her pussy.

"Hold tight, darlin'," he said gruffly. "I'm gonna fuck you hard and deep as punishment for disobeying me."

Briana bit back a smile. Those sorts of punishments she could take all day.

* * * *

Gus was in seventh heaven. She was so goddamned compliant, even though he knew she'd never done anything like this before. Oh, she'd masturbated often enough, but never with an audience. The fact that she'd so willingly put on a show for him had driven him wild. He placed one hand on her hips and guided her down onto him, parting her creamy folds with the fingers of the other hand and sliding smoothly into her. The vibrator had done nothing to stretch her narrow channel, but Gus wasn't complaining. His cock was more than capable of squeezing its way toward heaven without any artificial help.

"That's it, honey," he said gruffly, sliding deeper and closing his eyes as the walls of her cunt tantalized his sensitized cock. "Take it all."

"The butt plug, Master Gus. Shouldn't we remove it?"

"Nope. It stays."

She lowered her eyes. "As you wish."

Her willingness to please was Gus's undoing. He, Gus, and Fergal had been with any number of compliant women over the years, but Briana was in a class of her own. Sassy, smart, funny, and full of contradictions. She had no idea how attractive she actually was and didn't yet appreciate the full power of her femininity. Gus reckoned she must have had to fight the guys off with a big stick over the years but was too modest to say so. Okay, so she wasn't stick thin like a catwalk model, but what man would want to sleep with a woman who had no flesh on her bones? No enticing curves to tempt him?

Gus drove himself home with one powerful upward thrust, holding her hips to keep her in place. Not that she seemed particularly anxious to be anywhere else, but still.

"That's it, darlin'. You love my cock being inside you?"

"It feels heavenly," she replied, throwing her head so far back that her hair tickled his thighs.

"It'll get a whole lot better yet."

Holding her in place, Gus started moving, quickly picking up the pace, a pulsating warmth zipping between them. Briana, eyes still closed, moaned as he fucked her as hard and deep as he thought she could take it.

"You're so fucking tight, Briana. It's driving me insane."

"Master Gus, I—"

"Oh no. You just came once without my permission. You don't get to disobey me twice."

She leaned slightly forward, forcing him to change the direction of his thrusts, spoiling his undulating motion. He was now hitting the walls of her vagina rather than sinking all the way home. Her breasts brushed against his chest, and she removed one hand from the back of the couch to tweak his left nipple. Her arbitrary actions almost caused spontaneous combustion, and he knew she had him.

"Shit! Okay, darlin', as you were." She smiled seraphically and moved back to her previous position. "Let's do this."

Gus picked up the pace again, and Briana lowered her pelvis to meet his increasingly frantic upward thrusts. They were both panting, their bodies slick with perspiration, and he could see that Briana's pupils had dilated.

"Let it go, babe," he said as his balls tightened. With a groan and a sharp tap on her butt, he shot his load deep into the condom. At precisely the same moment Briana cried out and rode his cock like crazy, milking it like she was determined to extract every last ounce of pleasure from him that she possibly could.

"Hey, babe," he said, brushing his lips against hers when he finally stopped coming.

"Hey, yourself," she replied, her eyes still muddy with the residue of passion.

"What the hell are you doing to me?" he asked almost accusingly.

Chapter Fourteen

"Go sit by the fire," Gus said after he and Briana had showered together. "I'll just be a moment."

"Where are you going?"

Gus checked the camera feed on Harley's laptop. "Need to make absolutely sure we haven't had any uninvited guests."

"Is something wrong?"

"Not that I can see, but it's best to be thorough."

Gus pulled up his coat collar and whistled to Max. The two of them disappeared into the still-heavy rain, so Briana assumed he was looking out for Max's bathroom requirements while at the same time doing his security round. That was so typical of his considerate nature.

Left alone she felt soporific, totally satiated, barely awake, and very pleased with herself. These guys were teaching her so much about herself that she'd been completely unaware of, and she had loved every minute of her tuition so far.

Before she had time to miss Gus, he and Max returned. Gus removed his wet coat, Max made do with shaking his. Gus joined her on the sofa, and with her feet curled up underneath her, she rested her head on the hard, unyielding muscles of his chest. It was a little too comfortable, and she reminded herself not to get used to it. She was having fun but didn't delude herself that it was likely to be a long-term commitment on their part. Was that what she wanted it to be? Briana shook her head. No, that was crazy, impractical, and…well, impossible.

"Everything okay?" she asked.

"Yep. No one would be daft enough to come out here in this weather, but, like I said, we need to be ultracareful about your welfare, sugar."

She wasn't sure how to respond to that, and so she changed the subject. "Your family's in the restaurant business, right?"

"Yeah," he said. "Back in Tennessee."

"Why didn't you make a career of it, too? You easily could have done."

"My family wasn't happy when I enlisted. They just assumed I'd join the family business, like all my siblings did."

"Why didn't you?"

"If you'd met my dad you wouldn't ask that question. Controlling doesn't come close to describing his personality. We're too much alike and would have finished up killing each other."

She laughed. "Chef's knives at twenty paces."

Gus returned her smile. "Heads on chopping blocks, served medium-rare with a spicy dressing."

"Idiot!" She playfully thumped his arm. "You paint a grim picture, but presumably the rest of your family survives. I know you have a sister. Fergal told me about her."

Gus's eyebrows disappeared beneath his hairline. "Did he indeed?" He sent her a long, probing stare and then his generous mouth split into a wide smile. "I'll be damned!"

"What's the matter?"

"Fergal never talks about his disastrous marriage to my bitch of a sister and almost took my head off the last time I tried to get him to open up about it. God alone knows, he has reason enough to be bitter, but it ain't healthy to bottle it all up."

"You obviously have issues with your family."

"Only my father and sister. I have two older brothers who work in the restaurant, and we get along just fine."

"Fergal told me you felt guilty about him and your sister, but he doesn't blame you. Why would he?"

"Because I should have tried harder to warn him about Sheila. I already told you that my dad's a control freak and us boys were raised with the proverbial rod of iron. Sheila's the youngest, *and* his little princess. She learned to wrap him around her little finger from the get-go. Sugar wouldn't melt in her mouth, unless there was something she wanted and couldn't have. I told Fergal and Harley that she'd probably make a play for one of them when they came home with me one time. She's striking to look at and has learned to hide her manipulative personality over the years. Fergal was sucked in by her, and…well, I guess he told you the rest."

"Yes, she sounds selfish."

"She tried to put the blame on Fergal for her having strayed. The truth is, she couldn't bear to think of his attention being focused on anything or anyone other than her." Gus pulled a disgusted face. "Not even his career."

"Sounds like he's better off without her."

"No question, but it's left its mark, which is why I'm glad he spoke to you about it."

"I'm not sure why he did."

"Aren't you? You sure about that?" He sent her a look she couldn't interpret, lifted her head from his chest and stood up. "You stay there and doze. I need to start dinner."

"I'll help."

"I've got it."

Briana figured he didn't like anyone else intruding upon his space when he was in chef mode and so didn't insist. Besides, it was way too comfortable here and she was still boneless after their phenomenal sex fest. She yawned, snuggled into the cushions, and closed her eyes.

She awoke when she heard Fergal and Harley's voices.

"No one at home," Fergal replied to Gus's questioning look. "Any problems here?"

"Nothing I couldn't handle," Gus replied, looking smug as he pottered about in the kitchen.

Harley stopped to give Briana a brief kiss on the top of her head and disappeared into the bedrooms. Fergal sat beside her.

"You look…er, relaxed," he said, dropping a kiss on her lips.

"Gus has been entertaining me."

Fergal laughed. "I'll just bet he has."

"What happens now?" Briana asked. "About Greg and his father, I mean."

Fergal shrugged. "Not much we can do tonight, other than to keep a careful watch. At least the weather's on our side. I doubt if anyone will be tempted to come up here and try anything in this downpour, especially not if they know we're still here."

"I'll have a word with Raoul. See if they've found anything on the Seagrove guy yet," Harley said, rejoining them and giving Fergal an imperceptible nod.

"Do that," Fergal replied. "How long until dinner, Gus?"

"Ten minutes."

"Okay, babe." Fergal turned toward her and twirled one of her curls around his finger. "We've got time to kill while we wait out the weather."

Briana frowned. "You still think something bad will happen once the weather clears?"

"You need to accept that someone's out to destroy what you're doing here, darlin', and all my instincts tell me they're not about to stop anytime soon."

She swallowed down her apprehension. "All right, but it's not fair to ask you guys to hang around indefinitely."

Fergal flexed a brow. "Trying to get rid of us?"

"No, but it doesn't seem right. You're losing money by not being at work, and I can't afford to pay you."

"We're okay." Fergal's grin was pure sin. "If you want to pay us, we could play some more games while we wait. No pressure, though. If you'd rather not we won't walk out on you. Promise."

Briana was surprised to see an element of doubt creep into his expression. She'd never seen him anything other than totally in control and confident before. Eyes lowered, pussy leaking yet again, she was conscious of all three of them pausing with what they were doing, waiting to see how she'd respond. Did they honestly think she'd turn them down? She wasn't quite that masochistic.

"Yes please, Master Fergal," she said, eyes still downcast.

"Good girl." Gus resumed whatever he was doing in the kitchen. Harley's fingers flew over his computer keyboard again. "Harley just left some stuff in your room. Put it on, no deviations or additions, and join us back here as soon as you're ready."

She stood up, and Fergal patted her butt in dismissal. She was conscious of his eyes following her progress as she headed for the corridor leading to the bedroom. They clearly had something planned for her and had even taken the trouble to pick out the clothes they wanted her to wear. It would be something pretty and feminine, she was willing to bet. Guys liked women to look feminine, didn't they?

She entered her room and stopped dead in her tracks. *Oh my!* There were just two flimsy items of clothing laid out on the bed and a pair of four-inch heeled black sandals on the floor beside it.

"I can't wear those," she said aloud, picking up a pair of black latex crotchless panties and giggling. "And what the hell is this supposed to be?"

There was a honeycomb fishnet excuse for a dress lying on the bed. It would hide absolutely nothing, and if she wore it without a bra her tits would hang down to her knees. Still, they would know that because all three of them were already well acquainted with her large breasts and pretended to like them. She'd try the things on, just so that she could say that she had, and if necessary she'd go back out there and say *pollution*.

Hell, what was she thinking? Her disappointment would be ten times more severe than theirs if she called a halt to proceedings before they'd even gotten underway. Her juices were well and truly flowing, and she wanted to play this game of dress-up, even if it made her look ridiculous. She stripped off her clothes, sprayed herself all over with her favorite body perfume, and pulled on the panties. They were a snug fit, but the freedom of having her pussy lips and the crack in her ass uncovered was kind of liberating.

"Okay, so far so good," she told her reflection.

The dress was stretchy, with a high halter neck. She pulled it on and found it ended halfway down her thighs. It flattened her tits against her body, and the nipples poked out through holes in the honeycomb fabric. Hell, she'd felt sexy before, but this took the experience to new levels. Briana sat on the edge of the bed and slid her feet into the shoes. She wasn't surprised to find they were her size. Someone had done their research. She ran a brush through her hair and left it loose, the way they liked it. There was no point bothering with makeup since she was pretty sure they'd kiss lipstick right off her. Once she got heated up, mascara would trail down her face and make her look like a panda.

"Ready or not, here I come," she said, walking slowing toward the great room.

The sound of her heels on the wooden floor must have alerted them to her approach. All three men stood when she walked through the doorway and emitted a communal whistle of approval. They'd also transformed the room in her absence. Scented candles burned from every surface and soft music played from Harley's laptop.

"Dinner awaits, ma'am," Fergal said, extending a hand to her.

Harley held out her chair, which had a towel thrown over the cushion, presumably to protect it from her leaking cunt. These guys thought of everything.

"Thank you," she said, hamming up her role as lady since they appeared intent upon being gentleman. For now.

Gus served shrimp-and-avocado appetizers while Harley poured the wine.

"Did you learn anything more about Seagrove?" she asked.

"Nothing definitive," Fergal replied. "Zeke's still digging, but so far all he can find is that he runs a financial company back in Georgia."

Briana frowned, trying not to think about her tits resting on the edge of the table, nipples on clear display. "Why would a financial institution need a marketing company?"

Fergal laughed. "Honey, the financial services industry is in meltdown and needs all the help it can get."

"Everyone needs marketing help nowadays," Harley added. "Gotta love the internet."

Briana was getting used to having the guys around and felt comfortable with them. She was hungry and ate everything that was placed in front of her. Gus's cooking was so expert that she'd challenge anyone not to. The guys chatted to her about anything and everything, casting frequent glances at her near-naked body, but not once turning the conversation in the direction of the hot sex that she hoped would soon follow.

And the anticipation was driving her crazy.

Did they like what they saw or were they having second thoughts? This was a surreal situation, and she needed reassurance. None was forthcoming. Harley's laptop was on the table, and all three guys frequently glanced at the feedback from the outside cameras. There was nothing to see. The view didn't change, but that didn't stop them from looking at it with the same detached interest they spared for her. Briana no longer felt sexy. She felt neglected and unsure of herself.

Finally it came to an end. Fergal stood up and came round to help her from her chair. Instead of leading her back into the great room, as she'd expected him to do, he pulled her into his arms so forcefully that their bodies collided with a hard thud. Winded, she looked up into eyes rendered smoky with unmistakable desire.

"Do you have any idea how fucking sexy you look in that rig?" he asked.

"Actually no, since none of you have bothered to tell me."

Fergal laughed as his large hands moved down to cover the globes of her ass and pulled her against his hard-on. "Sometimes actions speak louder than words," he said. "Come on, we have a surprise for you."

She slid her hand into his, conscious of his vital strength transferring itself to her, washing away her uncertainties. Before she could take a step, her world went dark. Someone had blindfolded her. She gasped, taking a moment to adjust to the change. Fergal said nothing but kept hold of her hand. He moved forward and she moved with him, her excitement already enhanced by her inability to see anything at all.

"We're in the great room, Briana."

She nodded, aware of the warmth from the fire searing her back.

"Lie down on the comforter, honey. We have some more surprises for you."

Fergal guided her down and lay with her, his large, naked body snug against her side, his rigid cock resting on her thigh. His breath peppered her face as he captured her lips in a drugging kiss that sent her heightened senses reeling. His magical tongue worked its way into her mouth, and she matched his ravenous need taste for taste. She trembled with anticipation when another body landed on her opposite side and a trail of damp kisses were teasingly applied to her spinal column.

"Erogenous zones are found in the most unlikely places," Harley's hypnotic voice said from somewhere near her feet. She felt his hands on her legs forcing them apart. The material of the skimpy dress stretched but didn't tear as she bent her knees up for him. "My, that sure does look pretty," he said, blowing on her exposed pussy, sending her stomach into free fall with his wicked breath.

Fergal broke the kiss, and a moment later his hands were on her breasts, molding, caressing, his fingers probing until she thought she'd explode from sensory anticipation. She felt the need to move, to show him how much she was enjoying herself, but the other two were touching her as well and she didn't want to risk moving out of their range. Fergal sucked one pebbled nipple deep into his mouth, nipping at it with his teeth. She cried out as desperate pleasure spangled through her in unstoppable waves. Presumably Gus was the one behind her and his hand was now playing with her ass.

Three pairs of large hands appeared to be everywhere, driving her increasingly frantic, and she gave up trying to remember whose were where. She felt cool lube being squirted over her ass and this time tried real hard not to tense up when a finger invaded her anus. Someone—probably Gus—was doing something to her nipples. It pinched in a pleasurable sort of way.

"Nipples clamps," he said softly. "You like how they feel?"

"Yes, Master," she replied, writhing as renewed streaks of fiery sensation heated her bloodstream.

"That's good. There's another clamp, and Harley's gonna fix it on your pussy."

"He's what!"

"Just relax, sugar. It'll blow your mind."

Fergal's large hands sweeping across her gut and Gus sliding the plug into her butt distracted her. She barely felt it when Harley attached the clamp to her pussy lips. Presumably the three were connected by a chain because someone tugged at it and her entire world ignited.

"Guys, that's just awesome!"

"No one gave you permission to talk," Fergal said sternly.

"Sorry, Master Fergal."

"What happens to girls who talk out of turn, Briana?"

"They must be punished, Master Fergal."

"Then what do you have to say to me?"

"Please punish me for speaking without permission, Sir."

"Get on your hands and knees, darlin'."

She'd barely wriggled into position before a sharp crack across her ass caused Briana to cry out. Then she smiled as the most glorious sensations, aided by the plug in her butt, sent a disturbing thrill ricocheting through her bloodstream. The whip, or whatever Fergal was using, came down a second time, even harder. Someone tugged on the nipple clamps as it did so, which was one tantalizing tease too many. Shivers of liquid excitement plagued her body, and she seriously thought she'd come then and there.

"Don't you dare!" Damn it, Fergal really was a mind reader. "If you come, Briana, we'll remove the clamps and that ass plug you like so much. Then you'll be made to crouch in the corner for half an hour, with your butt on display, and no one will lay a finger on you."

Half an hour! I can't last half a minute without their hands. "Yes, Master," she said meekly, swallowing down her excitement and forcing her burgeoning orgasm back into its cage.

The next time he whipped her and someone tugged on the clamps, the other one pushed the butt plug a little deeper. They were testing her, trying to make her defy them and orgasm so they could punish her even more. Ha, she had their measure, and two could play at that game! She forced herself to think about all the poor manatees down in Florida who fell victim to careless boaters unable to read the warning signs and slow down. It helped, a little.

Fergal clearly sensed that she'd mastered her impulses because the whipping ceased and he nuzzled her neck instead. "Good girl," he said. "Self-control in these situations is an important thing to learn."

"Yes, Master."

"She's ready," Harley said.

"Okay, darlin'. If it gets too much, just remember the safety word."

If what gets too much? She felt a shifting of bodies around her and the plug being pulled from her butt. Someone tipped her onto her side and a muscled body slid down the length of her from behind. Slick fingers played with her anus and the head of a large cock pushed past her tight muscle.

"Open up for me, babe."

It was Fergal, his breath hot and heavy against her shoulder, as she did her best to relax. She was convinced he'd never fit and it would all be a waste of time. Hell, another body was now sliding down her front, tugging on the nipple clamps as a cock slid smoothly into her pussy.

"Room for two, darlin'?" Gus's voice asked.

Two? She couldn't possibly take them both at once. Surely that wasn't what they meant. But it appeared that they did. Fergal slid a little deeper into her backside. The sensation burned, but she was unwilling to have him stop, especially since Gus was making glorious progress into her cunt. The clamp was still attached to one of her pussy lips, pulling it tight, adding to the frenzy whirling through her brain—and other places. There was something different about Gus's cock. It felt harder, bigger.

"A cock ring," he told her. Really, these guys *had* to be mind readers. "Makes me last longer so I can love you deeper and harder."

He loved her?

"Don't leave me out, sugar."

Oh my! Harley was kneeling close to her face and tapped her lips with the tip of his cock. She opened her mouth and teased his head with her tongue, lapping up his salty pre-cum, enjoying the opportunity to tantalize him for a change as she sampled the devastatingly erotic taste of him. He groaned, confirming that her ploy was working better than she could have hoped. Momentarily distracted from Gus and Fergal, she was astonished to realize that the latter was now well inside her anus and that it no longer hurt. Quite the reverse in fact. The sensation was sharp, carnal, a delicious discovery. She pushed against him and received a tap on her thigh for her trouble.

"You need to keep absolutely still and let us do all the work," Fergal said. "I need to be careful back here. Don't want to hurt you."

She couldn't speak with Harley's cock halfway down her throat and nodded instead. She heard Fergal chuckle and had to suppress a groan when he withdrew almost all the way. Then she got it. He'd only done so in order that Gus might plunder her pussy. That was okay then. She returned to the important matter of giving Harley the best head she knew how, leaving Fergal and Gus to do what they did so damned well. Her nerve endings sang, she felt completely and absolutely consumed by them and was unsure where their bodies ended and hers began.

"That's it, babe," Fergal said, his voice throbbing with earthy vibrancy. "You've got us both now, you greedy little witch."

"She's got me and all," Harley said, his voice raw and edgy. "She's so fucking good at this."

"Yeah, and she's loving having her ass fucked," Fergal replied, taking his turn to drive into her.

Briana couldn't have made a verbal response, even if her mouth wasn't otherwise engaged. Her entire body was on fire with such desperate need that the spikes of lust shooting through her swamped all reason. They seemed so controlled, like they could keep this up all day, whereas she was coursing with readiness, with inexorable need, with an overwhelming determination not to be found wanting. Still, if they could hold out, so, too, could see.

She couldn't, of course. Fergal seemed determined that she'd crack before any of them. When he and Gus increased the rate and strength of their orchestrated thrusts, she felt herself on the cusp of something truly earth-shattering, and was sure she heard him chuckle with satisfaction, damn him. She sucked harder at Harley's cock. It jerked inside her mouth and he cursed.

"That's it, honey. Now you've got me. Shit, keep doing that thing with your tongue, angel. Don't worry about what those two goons are doing to you. Let's you and me party here." Briana sucked harder, running her tongue down the underside of his cock in the way that appeared to get to him, hitting his balls and tugging at the hairs on them with her teeth before reversing the process. "Fuck it, baby, here it comes."

Harley's cock pulsated in her mouth as she sucked it dry of his seed. Only then did she realize that Gus and Fergal had gone into overdrive and that her body was on fire. Really on fire. Harley slipped out of her mouth and she groaned aloud. It was too much. She absolutely had to come.

"I...I need..." She couldn't articulate the words, nor could she wait for permission, which she suspected would be withheld anyway. If they wanted a totally obedient partner they shouldn't have chosen a redhead. "Ohmygod!"

Her orgasm hit her broadside before she was ready to absorb it— so hot, so intense that her entire body quaked and turbulent heat coursed through her, spreading to her outermost places and then congealing in the pit of her stomach. She forgot all about remaining passive and pushed her hips between them, taking all she could get from one throbbing cock and then backing up to greedily extract as much as the other could offer her. It wasn't enough. Briana was flying without wings, transported to a place of carnal pleasure that she never wanted to leave. Nor would she until they had nothing left to offer her.

Only as the tremors finally started to fade did she realize that Fergal and Gus were still inside her, still rock hard.

"I think the lady just took advantage of our good natures," Gus said, chuckling.

"Fiendish punishments are whirling through my head," Fergal replied.

"Sorry, Masters," she said, trying not to laugh. The whole world should laugh with her. The world was a truly wonderful place. These were wonderful men. The new, sexually aware Briana was a wonderful person. What was there not to laugh about?

Fergal grunted and picked up the pace again. This time Briana remained passive as she felt them both expanding inside of her. She could smell their arousal, feel the perspiration on their skin, and willed them to have even half as good a time as she'd just experienced.

"You feel my cock fucking your ass?" Fergal asked in a tight voice. "You like that, darlin'?"

"Yes, Master Fergal, I love it. I love what Master Gus is doing to my pussy as well."

"Oh, I know you do, sweet thing," Gus replied. "You're a greedy little madam who can't get enough of our cocks. Am I right?"

"Yes, Sir."

"Come on then, honey. Let's see if we can make you sprout wings again."

They grunted as they worked her harder, and Briana gasped and welcomed the invasion of her body. She knew the precise moment when they were ready to explode. She noticed a fresh urgency in their inarticulate moans, felt their cocks thicken and twitch, felt her own body going into meltdown again.

"Shit, honey, let's do this," Fergal said from behind.

A gentler orgasm claimed her as both men's bodies shuddered, and she was acutely aware of their hot sperm shooting into condoms. She cried out as her body tingled with the pulsating warmth created by their sexual magnetism. Her last conscious thought before surrendering herself to the pleasure they'd given her—again—was to store every precious moment to memory.

Briana urgently needed to remember everything she'd experienced because she knew very well that this was a defining moment in her life. Nothing would ever top the deep, complete oneness she felt with these three wonderful men. She would never feel more desirable and feminine than she did at that moment. She also knew, without a shadow of a doubt, that she was in love with all three of them. What a joke! It was just plain greedy to love three men at once. Three men who'd be gone from here, probably within a matter of days.

Chapter Fifteen

Briana was carried to the shower, washed, kissed repeatedly, fussed over, complimented, and eventually dressed in a cozy robe.

"You okay?" Fergal asked for at least the fourth time as he carried her back to the great room and set her down on the couch. Harley handed her a restorative glass of wine. "We weren't too rough with you?"

"Hell no!" She sent each of them a reassuring smile. "That was totally unbelievable. You guys rock."

"Well, thank you, ma'am, we aim to please." Harley checked his computer screen. "No action," he said. "It's still pouring outside."

"I'll let Max out," Gus said.

The wind appeared to snatch the door out of his hands when he opened it. Briana shivered and pulled her robe more tightly about her. Harley noticed and threw another couple of logs on the fire.

"Can't have you catching cold, darlin'," he said, winking at her.

Gus came rushing back inside, tugging Max by the collar. "We've got a visitor," he said urgently. "Max spotted him. I just stopped him from going after him. I want that pleasure for myself."

Fergal and Harley reacted instantly, not wasting time with unnecessary questions. She was astonished when she saw handguns appear, seemingly from nowhere, as the three of them headed for the door.

"Stay here," Fergal said to her. "Lock the door behind us and don't open it unless you're sure it's us."

They were gone before she could respond. She did as they asked and shot the bolts across and then went to swap her robe for jeans and a sweatshirt. Who knew what she might be required to do? The guys had left Max with her, presumably for protection, but her dog pawed at the door, obviously wanting to have his turn at the intruder. Why hadn't they seen the person on Harley's screen if there actually was someone there? Max had probably caught onto the scent of a raccoon, or something. No strange cars had pulled up, but then if you were intent upon sabotage, Briana figured, you probably wouldn't advertise the fact by driving up to the door.

Where were they? She anxiously paced the length of the room, resisting the urge to grab a kitchen knife for protection. This was taking too long. She couldn't hear anything above the sound of the rain and the howling wind. What if one of them got hurt, or worse, trying to protect her? Briana shivered at the mere prospect, knowing she'd never forgive herself in that happened.

"Come on," she muttered, cuddling one of the kittens so tightly that he howled in protest and sprang from her arms.

After what seemed like forever but could only have been a few minutes, there was a sharp rap at the door.

"It's us," Fergal said. "Let us in."

Feeling totally relieved, Briana opened the door. All three of her men were bedraggled, but not nearly as much as the hapless guy they almost had to drag into the room with them.

"Meet Kyle Bruce," Fergal said glacially. "We just caught him trying to burn down the store with the roof timbers in it."

The guy looked ready to die of fright. "I didn't mean no harm," he said, sounding as pathetic as he looked.

"How could he burn anything down in this weather?" Briana asked.

"Honey, with the type of accelerant he had with him, anything would burn."

"Why?" Briana asked him. "Why are you doing this to me? I don't even know you."

"Answer the lady," Fergal said, giving him a hard jab in the back that almost sent him sprawling to the ground.

"Someone paid me. I have debts."

"Who paid you?" Harley asked.

Briana thought she knew the answer, even before Harley and Gus persuaded their captive to tell them.

"Greg Stone," he said in a grudging whisper.

Briana blinked. "Excuse me, don't you mean his father?"

Kyle looked confused. "Don't know nothing about his father."

"Why did Greg ask you to burn down the storage shed?" Gus asked.

"No idea. He said he had a score to settle and that no one would get hurt."

The guys exchanged a look that confirmed Briana's own thoughts. This was getting weirder by the minute.

"Take him into town," Fergal said to Gus and Harley. "Hand him over to the sheriff."

"Sure that's wise?" Gus asked. "We know the sheriff can't be trusted."

"He can't ignore attempted arson."

"No, look, please, I have a record." Kyle was almost begging. "If I get sent down for this—"

"Take him," Fergal said.

Gus and Harley left with the hapless Kyle in tow.

"What happens now?" Briana asked, hugging her arms around her torso, unable to get warm in spite of the blazing fire.

"We'll have a little chat with your friend Greg in the morning, see what he has to say for himself." Fergal looked pensive. "We still don't know why he's so keen to get his hands on this property. No offence, darlin', but it must involve more than wanting to get on your good side. He wouldn't be so destructive if that's what it was."

"Yes, I agree."

"I'll just be a minute, then we'll talk some more. There must be something we've overlooked."

"Where are you going?"

"We left the shed unsecured. I need to close it up and make sure our visitor didn't leave any other unwanted surprises for us." He touched her face. "You'll be okay for a couple of minutes?"

"Sure." She shook off his hand, not wanting to appear too needy. Not wanting him to go. "Go do what you have to do. Take Max with you. He probably didn't get to lift his leg when Gus took him out."

"Always thinking of everyone else's pleasure." He sent her an accusatory smile. "We're gonna have to teach you to think more about yourself."

"What makes you so sure I don't?"

"You don't, and won't, until you stop having negative thoughts about yourself. That's something else we're gonna have to work on." He ran a hand across her ass. "Don't go anywhere. I'll be right back."

Briana wandered around, too agitated to sit still as she waited for Fergal to return. Greg's betrayal cut her to the quick, even though it didn't especially surprise her. He always had been selfish and self-centered. Gus's description of his sister fitted Briana's view of Greg, although it had taken a lot of years for her to realize it. Greg was sweetness and light, just so long as people did things his way. She could still recall his incredulity, and then absolute fury, when she declined to marry him. It clearly hadn't occurred to him that she would reject him, and when she did, it took him a long time to accept that she was serious.

She went into the kitchen and grabbed an open bottle of wine from the fridge. If ever a situation called for Dutch courage, this was it. She heard the outside door open and breathed a sigh of relief. She'd always been self-sufficient, but tonight she didn't want to be on her own.

"That was quick," she said, turning around.

The glass slid from between her slack fingers, shattering on the flagstones of the kitchen floor when she looked up and saw a very wet, very angry-seeming Greg standing in front of her.

* * * *

Fergal and Max had to fight against the vicious wind to make their way to the shed. The door was still swinging open, and the timber nearest the opening was soaked. Fergal knew it would need to be moved farther undercover so it could dry out. With a frustrated sigh he set about lugging it, piece by piece, straining beneath the heavy loads. He laughed at Max. The dog had quickly lifted his leg and then run into the shed, clearly not enjoying getting wet.

"You're supposed to be a tough guy," he said to the mutt, glad to have saved Briana's timber, wishing he could resolve the rest of her problems with nothing more than a little sweat and muscle power. All his senses told him the danger wasn't past yet.

Damn it, he was furious with himself for underestimating Kyle and Greg. He was so keen for them all to play with Briana tonight that he'd convinced himself that her property wasn't in any danger during such a violent storm. A basic mistake he never should have made. And he wouldn't have, if he'd been thinking with his brain instead of his cock. If Kyle had arrived just half an hour earlier, they would still have been in the middle of their sex fest and he would have destroyed all this expensive timber—on Fergal's watch, too.

Well, at least they did manage to catch Kyle, more by luck than judgment, in the act. So what happened once they'd straightened Greg out and made him tell them why he wanted the place so badly? Well, they'd leave, obviously. Except the unthinkable had happened and Fergal didn't want to leave—not without Briana. And Briana's home was here. Fergal, Gus, and Harley didn't have emotional attachments to any piece of real estate. The same couldn't be said for a certain redheaded siren who'd made it her business to mess with his mind and sent his thoughts in a direction he'd never anticipated them taking again.

Fergal was a once-bitten-twice-shy type of guy and had vowed never to get serious about a woman. Briana had changed all that, and he was pretty sure Gus and Harley felt the same way about her. Perhaps a three-way commitment would be less likely to implode and would prove to be the catalyst that tempted Fergal to take a risk on a woman again. Whatever, he absolutely couldn't imagine a future without Briana in it. Fergal was in love again, and bolts of lightning hadn't struck him down for daring to make the admission.

Max stirred from the corner of the shed, cocked his head to one side, and started to bark frantically. He ran to the door, then back again, looking up at Fergal like he wanted to tell him something.

"I know it's still raining, bud," he said. "Not a lot I can do about that."

Max carried on barking like crazy. A rumbling growl echoed from his throat, and he pawed frantically at the ground.

"What the fuck?"

Cold fingers of fear wrapped themselves around Fergal's heart. Something wasn't right. Briana was in danger, and he'd been so absorbed thinking about her charms that he hadn't even sensed it. He abandoned the penultimate roof timber, allowing it to fall right where it was.

"Come on!"

He slammed the door to the shed behind him and Max and made for the house at a run.

* * * *

Briana felt her eyes bug out of her head. "What the hell—"

"Hey, Briana," Greg said, sauntering into the room. "How you doing?"

"Get out!" Briana yelled, wondering how he'd reached the house without any of them being aware. Wishing now that she *had* picked up that knife. She hadn't seen headlights, but he was soaking wet, so presumably he'd parked back down the track, out of sight, and hiked the rest of the way.

"Now that's not very friendly."

He strolled farther into the room, exuding confidence. His eyes were wild, his casual stance a poor disguise for his menacing intent. This obviously wasn't a social visit, and Briana admitted to herself that she was afraid of him. Why hadn't she kept Max with her? He'd never liked Greg, and Briana was starting to understand why.

"What do you want?"

"To see the love of my life, of course," he said with a cynical twist of his lips.

"Don't be ridiculous. Where's your car?"

"You always did underestimate me," he said, sounding slightly manic.

"What's to underestimate?" Briana knew it was stupid to antagonize him when he was obviously so unstable, but her famous temper wouldn't be quelled by an indulged bully who seemed to think she was afraid of him. She was, but she'd die before admitting it. She just needed to keep him talking until Fergus came back. "Far as I'm concerned, in your case, what you get is what you see."

His eyes darkened, and he took a step toward her. She was furious when she instinctively backed up a corresponding step. Fortunately he didn't attempt to touch her, mainly because he'd just glanced into the great room and his gaze fell on the rumpled comforter in front of the fire.

"Well," he said with a mocking glare. "I don't need to ask how you and your houseguests have been passing the time. Hope they got more out of the experience than I ever did. Personally, I found having sex with you akin to fucking a cold, unresponsive slab of meat."

Briana would once have been crushed by the insult and accepted the blame as a matter of course. She was no longer that person and sent him a quelling smile, imbuing it with a wealth of secret knowledge.

"Ever thought your own prowess might be to blame?" she asked sweetly.

Anger suffused his features. "Stop looking at the door, Briana. There's no one here except you and me. That idiot I sent up here got himself caught. I saw your friends driving him back down the track and leaving you here all by your little self. I figured they might catch him, that's why I came up to keep an eye on him." He huffed. "I don't know, you just can't get the help nowadays. If you want a job doing, it's best to do it yourself."

"What job *do* you want doing, Greg? Why are you so desperate to get your hands on this place?" Hopefully he wouldn't be able to help boasting and it would buy her the time she needed. "You never even liked it, far as I recall."

"Ah, well, that was before I found out a deposit of bentonite sits right below your pretty little piece of paradise."

"Of course!"

Briana clapped a hand across her mouth. There was already a thriving bentonite industry in the area, but Briana had no idea there was actually a deposit close to her grandmother's land. Thinking about it, Gran had said something about hydrology and vegetation studies taking place just before she died. Briana should have made the connection but had just assumed the environmental groups had commissioned them to keep their records of the area current. It had happened before.

"You'd never get permission to mine up here," she sneered. "It's a protected area."

Greg cocked a brow. "You sure about that?"

She recalled Fergal saying that Greg's father probably had half the commissioners in Valley County in his back pocket. Elections were due soon. Presumably Greg and his father couldn't be sure that their men would get reelected, hence their haste.

"Your daddy must be real proud of you."

Greg curled his lips. "He doesn't know what I'm doing. I plan to surprise him when it's all tied up."

Briana hid her surprise behind a mocking façade. "Hope he's got a lot of patience."

"I begged for the opportunity to make more decisions within the company," Greg said, explaining his situation even though she hadn't asked. "He was too stuck in his ways. We needed to take on higher-risk, higher-return clients, which is what I did when he finally gave me a free hand." He glowered at nothing in particular. "How was I to know the fucking economy would tank?"

"Ah, I get it. You've bankrupted his company and now want to prove to him that your genius lateral thinking can save the day." She released a hollow laugh. "Grow up, Greg. You won't get permission to mine up here if I object, which obviously I will."

"Precisely." Greg sent her a toxic grin that frightened the shit out of her. "Shame you went out looking for your dog in this storm, lost your footing, and fell in the lake."

Come on, Fergal!

Briana simply shook her head. "It ain't gonna happen."

She'd let her guard down and he obviously sensed it. Before she could stop him, he thrust out a hand and grabbed her arm. Briana tried to smash her knee into his groin, but he moved back and her blow merely glanced off him.

"Not a big enough target," she said, trying for bravado when she was actually petrified.

He hit her face hard just as the door flew open and Fergal and Max bounded through it. Relief coursed through her as Max flew toward Greg. Greg moved behind her and threw a strong arm around her neck, almost cutting off her windpipe and Max's ability to get near enough to bite him.

"Back off," he said, "and get that fucking mutt out of here."

Fergal regarded him with murder in his eyes. He stood stock-still, legs slightly apart, and appeared to assess the scene with total clarity. His calmness clearly got to Greg.

"I said lose the dog."

Fergal opened the door again and had to force Max outside.

"What the fuck are you doing here anyway?" Greg asked. "I just saw you two guys drive down the track."

"Stop being such a fucking coward, hiding behind a woman, and face me like a man. Or don't you have the stones for it?"

"If you hadn't interfered, all this would be sorted by now."

Briana didn't know what to do, but there had to be something. She could sense Greg's desperation in the strength of the stranglehold he'd put on her. Fergal clearly didn't underestimate him, and she could also sense his frustration. She saw the knife that she'd been tempted to grab as a weapon earlier, sitting on the chopping board just behind her, a few tantalizing inches away from her hand. If she could just nudge Greg in that direction. She slanted her eyes sideways, praying that Fergal would get the message.

She gauged the exact moment when he did. He moved diagonally a step or two toward the surface. Greg instinctively pulled Briana that way, in order to maintain the distance between them. She could hardly breathe, so tight was Greg's hold on her neck, and spots danced in front of her eyes. If she didn't move now then she might well pass out. She inhaled as much air as her restricted windpipe would permit and then sagged against Greg's body. The move clearly surprised him, and he released his hold, just fractionally. Fergal sprang forward at exactly the same moment as Briana grabbed the knife and stuck it into Greg's thigh.

"Argh! Fucking bitch!"

He released her and pulled the knife free. With her debilitated strength she hadn't plunged it nearly deeply enough. Greg's eyes were black with rage, and he lunged for her. His fingers brushed against her arm, but before he could grab it, Fergal's fist made bone-crunching connection with Greg's face. Blood spurted from his nose as he crumpled to the floor, cursing and screaming, landing on the remnants of Briana's wineglass.

Chapter Sixteen

"You okay, babe?"

Fergal could see that Greg wouldn't be getting up anytime soon, and so his immediate concern was for Briana. She staggered out of the kitchen and fell into a chair, still struggling to breathe. Her face was deathly pale, apart from the angry welts left on her cheek by Greg's hand. Fergal felt a murderous rage toward the sniveling coward crumpled on the floor, but he'd deal with him in a moment.

"Let me look at you." He crouched beside Briana, pulled her hair away from her neck and let forth with a string of curses in the variety of the languages he'd learned in the service. There were ugly marks on her neck where the son of a bitch had held her so tight. She'd be badly bruised, but not as badly as Stone would be when Fergal had finished with him.

"I'm okay," she replied. "I just need a minute."

"Take all the time you need, honey." Fergal ran a hand soothingly down her back. "It's all over now."

"He told me…He told me that—"

"It's okay. Tell me later. I'll get some ice for your neck."

"What about me?" Greg whined when Fergal walked past him. "I'm bleeding here."

"Think yourself lucky you're still fucking breathing."

Fergal grabbed a dish towel, filled it with ice, and went straight back to Briana, savagely kicking Greg's leg out of his way.

"Here, wrap this around your neck, honey." Her hands were trembling so he did it for her. "I never should have left you alone," he said, quietly seething at his own stupidity.

"It's okay."

Fergal glanced again at her injuries. "Like hell it is!"

A scratching sound reached their ears. "Let Max in, will you? He's probably cold."

"Don't let that fucking mutt get anywhere near me." Greg's petulant whine made him sound like he had a head cold. Fergal took considerable satisfaction from the fact that he'd obviously broken his nose when he hit him. *Should have broken his fucking useless neck.*

Fergal shot him a look. "Don't tempt me."

Max barreled into the room as soon as Fergal opened the door, teeth bared, tail quivering, a deep growl rumbling in his throat. He headed straight for Greg. Fergal was sorely tempted to let Max tear the jerk's throat out, but called him off at the last possible moment. The dog obeyed him with obvious reluctance, backing off but keeping a weather eye on Greg and maintaining a continuous growl. Greg staggered to his feet, and Max's growls grew louder. Greg was so scared of the dog that Fergal figured he might just do something stupid. He needed to give Briana his full attention, smother her with kisses, and apologize for letting her down. But he couldn't—not until Greg had been neutralized.

"I'll just deal with the trash, darlin'," he said to Briana. "Won't be but a minute."

He grabbed Greg by the back of his collar and threw him with considerable force into a hard kitchen chair.

"Hey, careful. I'm bleeding here."

"You'll live, unfortunately."

Fergal found a length of strong cord in one of the kitchen drawers and tied Greg's hands behind him tight enough to make him wince. Then he grabbed his cell and called Harley.

"How's it going?" he asked. "Any problems?"

"The sheriff has just locked Bruce up. He didn't want to but had no choice, given that we caught him red-handed. I still think he's trying to decide what to do, though."

"He's thinking about his own hide, presumably."

"That's my take."

"His mind's just been made up for him. Get back here and bring him with you. We have another prisoner for him."

Fergal briefly filled Harley in on events.

"We're on our way," Harley said curtly, cutting the connection.

Fergal went back to Briana, who seemed to have regained a little color. "Not long now, babe," he said, rubbing her hands between his. "Harley's bringing the sheriff out here with him."

"That's good." Greg's nasal voice caused them both to turn and look at him. "Then I can press charges against you two for assault and false imprisonment."

Fergal actually laughed. "Yeah, right."

"I came out here out of the goodness of my heart to check on Briana 'cause the weather was so bad and I was worried about her. She invited me in and then you barged in and attacked me in a jealous rage." Greg looked as though he actually believed the sheriff would buy his story. "Everyone knows Briana's my girl. I'll be believed."

Briana drew an indignant breath. "That's bullshit," she said. "No one invited you in. You attacked me, and I have the bruises to prove it."

"Could have gotten them some other way. Looks like you and lover boy here have been having quite a party." He nodded toward the comforter. "No, make that three lover boys. When the locals hear about your sluttish behavior, any sympathy they might otherwise have felt will switch to me. Course, the sheriff will be on my side, anyway. He fucking well ought to be. I pay him well enough."

"I'm not gonna tell you again, asshole. Shut the fuck up!"

Fergal stood over Greg, fists clenched. It took every ounce of his military training not to knock that smug smirk off his bloodied face. Instead he turned his back to him and returned to Briana's side. In an undertone she repeated everything Greg had told her about his reasons for wanting the lodge.

"He's right," she said in a concerned voice. "The locals will take his side if he puts a positive spin on it and he has the sheriff in his corner. His father wields a lot of power around these parts."

Fergal was filled with rage. "He won't get away with it while I still have breath in my body, darlin'." He took her hand and traced patterns on her palm with the pad of his thumb. "He's pissing in the wind. Don't let him get to you. It's what he wants."

Gus, Harley, the sheriff, and one of his deputies arrived shortly after that. Fergal stood to let them in. Gus and Harley made straight for Briana, fussing over her. The sheriff looked at the state of Greg and scowled.

"What happened to him?"

"This fucking animal broke my nose, that's what."

Greg went into his spiel about having been attacked by Fergal. It was obvious that the sheriff was still vacillating, and the longer Greg spoke, the more likely it appeared that he'd come down on his side. Fergal took Harley and Gus aside and told them what had really happened.

"Problem is, we can't prove it."

Harley laughed. "Sure we can. Briana, tell the sheriff what Greg told you."

She did so in a clear, concise voice.

"Your word against mine, sweet thing," Greg said smugly.

"Not precisely." Harley stepped forward. "What time did Greg burst in on you, Briana?"

"Just before ten. Why?"

Without responding, Harley went to a shelf in the great room and removed a small device. "Ten o'clock, you say." He pressed a few buttons, and Greg's voice came through loud and clear, condemning himself with his own words.

Fergal glanced at Greg and took considerable satisfaction when the color drained from his face and his head fell forward in defeat.

"A voice activated recorder," Harley said. "Two hundred hours of recording space, long battery life, available from all good retailors in your area."

Gus laughed. "Sure you don't want to change your story, Stone?"

Greg's language would have made a sailor blush when the sheriff exchanged the cord binding his hands for police-issue handcuffs.

"Shit, Harley," Fergal said, slapping his back. "You should have told me about that."

"You know me," he said, shrugging. "I do like my gadgets and I also like to be prepared. I just forget to mention this little baby, is all."

Briana stood up and wrapped her arms around Harley's neck once the sheriff had relieved them of their unwanted guest. "Now I know you really are clever," she said, kissing him.

"I did tell you that, sweetheart."

"Come on, honey," Fergal said. "Let's get you in the bath and then into bed. You've had quite a day."

"There's a lot we need to talk about."

"Not now. One of us will stay with you if you like, but only to make sure you sleep." He kissed her brow. "Tomorrow we'll talk."

* * * *

Briana did sleep. Thanks to the solidity of Fergal's muscled body spooned behind hers, holding her all night, making her feel safe, she slept like a baby and didn't have a single bad dream. Fergal's rigid cock pressing against her back woke her sometime after sun up.

"Hmm," she said, stretching in his arms and shooting him a smile. "Seems like you're pleased to see me."

"Sorry about that. Can't seem to help myself when you're around, but it's inappropriate, given what you've been through."

"That way the bad guy wins."

"He almost fucking did, thanks to my neglect. If Max hadn't warned me, I—"

"Shush." She wriggled in his arms until they were face to face. "No way in this world would I have allowed him to throw me into the lake. I'm not quite that biddable."

"How would you have stopped him? He's twice your weight."

"Oh, I don't know." She plunked at her lower lip with her index finger, pretending to think about it. "Perhaps I'd have gone all weak and girly on him, then kneed him in the nuts."

Fergal laughed, but she could see he was still beating himself up. She took matters into her own hands and instigated a slow kiss that fired her passions.

"Still," she said when she broke it. "If you're still feeling bad, I can think of ways you could make it up to me. It would be a damned shame to let such a fine hard-on go to waste."

"Witch!"

Fergal threw her onto her back and put his capable hands to good use. He gave her a mind-blowing orgasm with his lips, then another with his gorgeous cock buried deep inside her. She was so boneless afterwards that he had to carry her to the shower, where he took it upon himself to wash every inch of her so slowly, with such sensuous sweeps of his hands, that she was ready to go another round.

"Uh-uh." He shook a finger at her. "We need to catch up with the others."

Hand in hand, they joined Gus and Harley for a late breakfast.

"The sheriff called," Gus said. "He needs us all to go into town and make statements. Greg's father's gotten his son the best lawyer his limited funds can provide, but no way will he wriggle out of this one."

"The sheriff is falling over himself to come down on our side," Harley said, the curl of his upper lip mirroring Fergal's own disdain.

Seth and Maurice accosted them as soon as they left the sheriff's office several hours later, keen to hear all the details firsthand.

"The whole town's abuzzing with the news of Stone's downfall," Seth said gleefully as they all shared a pot of coffee outside the barber shop.

"Did the cocky so-and-so really think he could get away with mining out your way?" Maurice asked.

"Seems so," Briana replied, shrugging. "Desperate men and all that. He's been raised to believe anything he wants he can have, so why wouldn't he?"

"Well then, young lady, it's a good job we told your daddy you could use some help."

"Just don't expect me to thank you," she replied, shaking a finger at them both but clearly trying not to laugh.

"We'll thank you for her," Gus said.

"What worries me," Briana said wistfully, "is how to stop other people trying to do the same thing. Now that it's common knowledge there's bentonite beneath my land, there's no telling what tricks people might try to get licenses to mine. I'll never have a moment's peace."

"I've been thinking about that," Fergal replied. "There's been a bit of local media interest in Stone's spectacular downfall, right?"

"Right," Seth agreed, chuckling. "Wonder how them vultures found out about it so damned quick?"

Fergal cocked a brow. "I can't begin to imagine. Which is the leading paper in this valley?"

"*The Glasgow Courier*," Seth and Maurice replied before Briana could.

"Well then, I think I have a plan."

* * * *

Two days later Fergal and his buddies watched Briana being interviewed by the *Courier*'s leading feature writer. She conducted him all over the lodge, showed him a lot of her photographs of the local wildlife, flora and fauna, and explained her plans for the place. She couldn't say too much about Greg and his multifarious scheme since a court case against him was pending. Fergal knew the reporter would join the dots and that his feature would have the environmentalists up in arms.

Briana's little piece of paradise was safe.

Their job was done, and Fergal knew they had no reason to linger. Even so, they spent another week finishing Briana's roof and helping her knock the inside into shape. Harley helped her create a website advertising the place, again using her own photographs as promotion.

Every night they carried on with her erotic education. Her sensuality and vigorous enthusiasm continued make dents in Fergal's battered heart. He knew his buddies expected for him to pull out of the area any day. He could sense that Briana expected them to leave as well. There really was no reason for them to stay.

Except there was every reason.

"Guys," he said one afternoon when Briana was running errands in town. "We need to talk."

"About fucking time," Harley said, grinning.

When Briana returned home, Gus already had supper cooking. Once they'd eaten, Fergal led Briana back into the great room, but instead of the sex games she'd probably been expecting, he sat her down.

"We need to talk," he said, repeating the words he'd said to Gus and Harley a few hours earlier.

"About what?" she asked, sharing a glance between the three of them. "Are you leaving?"

"Well, we do need to—"

"I realize that. I'm grateful that you've stayed for so long, but I know you have a business to run back in Columbia Falls."

"That's true, and—"

"You don't need to worry about me anymore." She was no longer making eye contact with any of them, and Fergal dared to hope that was because she didn't actually want them to leave. It was hard to tell with Briana because she played her cards close to her chest. Presumably that was the result of growing up with no mother and an absentee father. "Everything's on track here. I'm already receiving tons of inquiries from the website and the newspaper articles and really, I—"

"Shut up, Briana." Fergal took her hand. "We'll leave if you really want us to, but we were rather hoping you'd ask us to stay."

"Stay!" Her eyes flew wide open and finally her gaze locked with Fergal's. "But what about—"

"We can lead treks here just as easily as we can in Columbia falls—"

"And we can teach punters to dive in the lake," Gus added.

"We thought you could offer walks for those who are into photography," Harley said, briefly touching her cheek.

Fergal nodded. "With our combined skills the four of us could make a real go of this place."

Tears slid down her face. "Thanks, guys, I appreciate the offer, really I do, but it wouldn't work."

"Why not?" all three of them asked together.

"Well, if you want to know the truth, I love all three of you equally."

"That's good to know. We weren't sure how you felt about us," Fergal said, "but we all love you."

"Ah, but it doesn't work that way. One woman could never keep three hunks like you happy for long, and I'd rather part with you all now than experience the agony of seeing you with other women."

"And just what makes you think you couldn't keep us happy?" Gus asked. "You've done a bang-up job of it so far."

"Oh, come on, Gus, I just happen to be convenient." She looked away, tears shimmering. "A permanent relationship is a different matter altogether."

"Some bastard really knocked your self-confidence," Fergal said softly. "I know Stone blamed his own inadequacies on you but what did that jerk in Florida do to you, honey? All you've ever said is that it didn't work out."

She hesitated for a long time before responding. "He dumped me for another girl on the project, if you must know. A slimmer, sexier girl."

All three of them laughed. "Then he was a jackass, and you're better off without him," Harley said.

"You are sex on legs, darlin'," Fergal said. "Never doubt it for a moment."

She still seemed reluctant to accept what they told her was the truth. "You all really believe that?"

"What do we have to do to convince you that we love every inch of you?" Harley asked, grabbing her shoulders.

"Even my freckles?"

"Especially those," Gus replied. "My personal favorites are the line across your belly, just above—"

"Military guys are different," Fergal said. "We all enlist for different reasons but once we've seen combat we're never quite the same again. Hell, some of the places we've been and the shit we've witnessed, we'd be freaks if it *didn't* affect us. Bottom line, all of us want a normal family life but none of us are prepared to go it alone. We need you to make us whole, normal human beings again a damned sight more than you need us."

"We're damaged goods, darlin'," Harley added. "And only you can make us whole."

"Will you do it, sweet thing?" Fergal asked. "Are you prepared to take the chance on us making you happy for the rest of your life?"

Tears streamed down her face when the enormity of what they were asking clearly struck home.

"You're really serious about this, aren't you?"

"Never more so," Gus replied for them all. "We want to build a life with you."

"We want to grow old with you," Harley added.

"Then I'd be a fool to turn you down."

"We'll make sure you never regret it," Fergal said.

She nodded, tentatively at first, and then so hard her head must have spun. "Yes!" she cried. "Yes, please."

Epilogue

Three Months Later

"Hey, look at this," Raoul said, beckoning Zeke over to his computer.

"What you got, bud?"

"See for yourself."

Zeke looked over Raoul's shoulder at the photo of their three former Montana operatives. They appeared fit, tanned, and sported goofy grins as they formed a protective semicircle around Briana Redmond.

"They sure do look happy."

"Fergal says they're all set to open their lodge and are booked up already a year in advance."

"That's good."

"Yeah." Raoul stretched his arms above his head. "But remind me not to send our best operatives to rescue ladies in distress again. That's twice now that they've finished up getting permanently involved, leaving us with gaps to fill in our organization."

"Can't hold it against the guys if they've found what they've been looking for."

"Still, it's a pain in the ass, having to train their replacements."

Zeke slapped Raoul's shoulder as they headed for the door, preparing to do precisely that with the half-dozen guys they'd selected as possible new recruits.

"And you enjoy every moment of it, buddy. You can't fool me."

"Yeah, yeah."

"Still," Zeke mused. "Doesn't it make you wonder if we're missing something? I mean Fergal, Gus, and Harley were confirmed bachelors. I'd have bet good money that no one woman could ever keep them happy. Looks like I was wrong."

"And your point is?"

"Just sayin'," Zeke replied mildly. "Perhaps we're missing out."

"Feel free to look any time you feel the need," Raoul said. "Me, I'm perfectly happy as I am."

Zeke rolled his eyes. "Sure you are, buddy. Sure you are."

THE END

WWW.ZARACHASE.COM

ABOUT THE AUTHOR

Zara Chase is a British author who spends a lot of her time travelling the world. Being a gypsy provides her with ample opportunities to scope out exotic locations for her stories. She likes to involve her heroines in her erotic novels in all sorts of dangerous situations—and not only with the hunky heroes whom they encounter along the way. Murder, blackmail, kidnapping, and fraud—to name just a few of life's more common crimes—make frequent appearances in her books, adding pace and excitement to her racy stories.

Zara is an animal lover who enjoys keeping fit and is on a one-woman mission to keep the wine industry ahead of the recession.

For all titles by Zara Chase, please visit
www.bookstrand.com/zara-chase

Siren Publishing, Inc.
www.SirenPublishing.com

CPSIA information can be obtained at www.ICGtesting.com
Printed in the USA
LVOW04s0639140415

434403LV00022B/645/P